A VERY COOKIE CHRISTMAS

A HEARTSPRINGS VALLEY WINTER TALE (BOOK 2)

ANNE CHASE

THOMAS PUBLISHING

ISBN: 1945320036

ISBN-13: 978-1945320033

For my parents

CHAPTER 1

*A*n insistent *beep-beep-beep*, familiar yet unwelcome, roused Clara from unconsciousness. Instinctively, she burrowed deeper under the covers, trying desperately to slip back into much-needed slumber.

But her alarm clock wasn't in an accommodating mood. It sounded angrier than usual, like it was chastising her for preferring sleep over everything else the day had in store for her.

With a groan, she remembered: The day had *a lot* in store for her. Eyes still firmly shut despite the clock's nagging, she inched her face from under the covers and steeled herself for the inevitable. The instant she opened her eyes, she'd see almost everything there was to see in her tiny Brooklyn studio apartment: the cracked plaster on the walls, the worn hardwood floor, the water stain on the ceiling next to the big old windows that leaked cold air like a sieve. She'd also see her mismatched furniture: the rattan couch donated by a friend, the bland cherry-wood coffee table she'd found on the sidewalk, and the tiny cafe table, bought cheap from a thrift store, that did double-duty as desk and dining table. The only truly personal touches — the only things that demonstrated that she, Clara Cane, was the occupant of this dismal space rather than some other ambitious young workaholic — were the photographs of family and friends she'd brought with her when she moved in, which she'd hung in a framed group on the wall near the entry door.

With a sigh, she accepted her fate and pushed her blanket from her face. The pre-dawn light confirmed that exactly nothing had changed since she'd collapsed exhausted in her bed five hours earlier. But her brow furrowed as she realized the light filtering through the curtains seemed brighter than it should be. She swiveled her head to her alarm clock and gasped.

It was 6:23 a.m.!

She bolted upright. How was that possible? She'd set the clock for 6:00 a.m. sharp — she was sure of that. Had she actually slept through *twenty-three minutes* of that insistent beeping?

She leaped out of bed and turned off the alarm, already grappling with how to compress forty-five minutes of standard morning prep into exactly twenty-two minutes of panicked scrambling.

She raced into the shower, praying as she lathered up that the building's ancient water heater would show her some mercy. On this morning of all mornings, the last thing she needed was —

Aaaggh! A shocking blast of ice-cold water slammed into her, turning her lovely hot shower into an arctic dunk tank. She pushed the stream of frigid water away from her shivering body and, heart racing, waited for the heat to return. When it did, a few seconds later — the boiler liked to keep the residents guessing — she finished up as quickly as possible.

A moment later, wrapped in a towel and shivering in front of the bathroom mirror, the thought came: Perhaps the water heater — or the universe in general — was trying to tell her something. Maybe it was doing its darnedest to tell her that paying too much rent for a drafty fourth-floor studio walkup wasn't such a great idea.

If so, the water heater (or universe) was right. But she'd have to ponder that later — after she caught her bus. She looked at the frowning face in the mirror. Her honey-brown, shoulder-length hair would get a day of rest from her typical blow-dry/straightening routine. She'd also have to take a pass on the blush and lip gloss she normally applied to face the world.

Quickly, she stepped out of the bathroom and

threw on the casual traveling clothes — jeans, tee shirt, NYU sweatshirt, and winter boots — she'd selected the previous night while packing. With a final glance around her apartment — which she hadn't even tried to decorate for Christmas, she realized sadly — she shrugged into her heavy winter coat, grabbed her phone and suitcase, and headed out.

Ten minutes later, as her subway train rattled through the dark tunnel toward Manhattan, she glanced at her phone and saw — the darn thing was nearly dead! How could she have forgotten to plug it in? Two percent battery power would not last long. When her boss called with his normal flood of questions and instructions — and he would, even though she'd reminded him a million times that she was heading home for Christmas — what was she going to do? There was no time to find an outlet to juice it back up, thanks to those extra twenty-three minutes of slumber. No time for her morning mocha latte, no time to collect her thoughts, no time for anything other than rushing to catch her ride home.

She dashed toward her bus when she reached the terminal, hopping aboard mere seconds before the driver shut the door and pulled away. The bus was packed with holiday travelers like herself, eager to flee the big city and return home for Christmas. She slipped into the last available seat, next to a big sleeping guy who overflowed from his seat into hers.

The man was snoring softly, oblivious to her and the world. As carefully as she could, she settled in and willed herself to relax as the bus emerged onto the busy streets of Manhattan and began its long journey north into New England.

In five hours, she would be back in her hometown of Heartsprings Valley. Free, at least for a few days, from the frantic energy of the big city and the stress and tension of her busy job.

As if on cue, her phone vibrated. She looked at it and sighed. Her boss, Nigel Farraday, was a public relations genius — legions of grateful clients attested to that — but a wreck when it came to organizing himself.

Clara picked up. "Good morning, Nigel."

"Where is my laptop?" Nigel said, his crisp British accent laced, as usual, with frantic worry.

Clara bit her lip to suppress a smile. She could picture him standing in his study, hand running through his thinning hair, a frazzled look on his face, eyes darting wildly around the room as he looked for his missing computer.

"Next to the printer. Remember? We plugged it in there, to make sure it's charged for your flight."

"Right," he said. "My tickets?"

"In your phone. You have your phone, right?"

"Of course. What do you think I'm talking to you with?"

"And it's charged up?"

A pause, then: "Ten percent."

"Plug it in when you can. My own phone is down to two percent, and I'm already on the bus, so I might not be reachable for a few hours."

"Fine," he said. "Just make sure Melody is taken care of."

An alarm bell, similar in unpleasantness to the one next to her bed, went off in her head. Melody Connelly, their newest client, was not only a Broadway star, a singer-dancer-actress of dazzling ability, but also a demanding diva whose flights of fancy had driven Clara to distraction during their brief time working together.

"What do you mean, taken care of?" Clara said, a tingle of dread creeping up her spine.

"On her little Christmas jaunt," Nigel said.

Clara's heart climbed into her throat. "*What* little Christmas jaunt?"

"Didn't I tell you? She's trying to snag a cooking show, which means she needs to be seen as more relatable — less 'big-city' and more 'small-town-girl' — so I suggested she visit one of those quaint New England villages where everything is delightful and cheerful and homey so she can meet rustic locals and have heartwarming conversations with them. On camera, of course. You know what I mean."

"No, I don't know what you mean," Clara said, trying hard not to crush the phone to pieces in her hand.

"She loved the idea, of course. She'll be there this afternoon."

"She'll be *where* this afternoon?"

"Your little town. Whatsitsname."

"She's coming to *Heartsprings Valley*?"

"Yes, exactly. Such an adorable name. You'll need to book her into one of those charming little inns they have up there. I'm sure there's one of those — isn't there always?"

Clara closed her eyes and willed herself not to scream at her boss while sitting in a bus filled with dozens of sleeping strangers.

She opened her eyes and looked at her phone. Power left: one percent. That was about how much patience she had left, too.

"Nigel," she said, struggling to keep her voice quiet and even. "You didn't tell me about any of this."

"Oh," Nigel said. "Sorry. But it's no problem, not for you. You have my full confidence. You know I'd be nowhere without you, dear. Clara Cane, assistant extraordinaire, Girl Friday and Wonder Woman rolled into one. The visuals from Melody's holiday jaunt will be delightful — we'll post them everywhere. Just the thing to broaden her brand."

Clara let out a sigh. Really, should she be surprised? Nigel was just being Nigel — scattered and forgetful and insightful, all at the same time. It helped, of course, that he appreciated her and her hard work. She'd learned so much from him in two years as his assistant.

"Fine," she said. "I'll take care of her."

"That's my girl," he said. "What time is my flight?"

"Your flight's in three hours," she said. "You need to leave now, with your phone and passport and computer, and take a cab to JFK."

"Which airport, did you say?"

"JFK."

"Where's my passport?"

"In your valise. Where we put it last night."

"Thank you, dear girl. I don't know what I'd do without you. You are a treasure. I hope you have a very merry Christmas."

"Merry Christmas, Nigel," she replied. "Give my best to Pamela and the kids."

"Ta ta for now."

And he was gone. She took a deep breath and exhaled slowly. It was her fervent hope that Nigel's wife and kids — he was joining them on St. Barts for the holiday — would keep his phone out of his hands for at least a few days.

That was all she wanted, really. A few days of relaxation back home, just her and her dad. Of all the Christmas gifts she could receive, peace and quiet were what she wished for most.

Along with sleep.

Yes, sleep!

She shut off her phone and took another deep

breath. It would be simple enough to book Melody into the Heartsprings Valley Inn, and easy to find her a few Christmas activities. Chances were the Broadway diva would tire of small-town life quickly and flee back to the big city. With a bit of preparation, Clara could keep Melody out of her hair and still have the easy, worry-free, sleep-filled Christmas she so desperately needed.

As if to challenge that thought, the big snoring man next to her shifted in his seat and flung a meaty arm onto her lap. With a frown, she took hold of the arm and carefully repositioned it on top of the man's expansive belly.

Peace and quiet and sleep, here I come, she thought. *Please please please....*

CHAPTER 2

*C*lara felt her excitement rising as she stared out the window at the increasingly beautiful winter scenery. The bus was nearly empty now, most passengers having already reached their destinations.

Almost home. A rush of warmth and longing overtook her. They were about twenty minutes away, on the two-lane road that led over the mountain ridge into Heartsprings Valley. Fresh snow blanketed the thick stands of cedar that ran up and down the hills. Through the trees, she caught glimpses of farmhouses and barns, many of them decorated with holiday lights and ornaments. As the bus rounded a bend, she grinned at a snowman standing proudly by the side of the road, his arms raised in greeting, a black top hat on his head, a red scarf around his neck, and a corncob pipe in his smiling mouth.

She missed her hometown. She missed it a lot.

Back in high school, she'd been so impatient to leave, so eager to prove herself in the big wide world. In college in New York, she'd convinced herself that her future lay in that vast metropolis. Maybe her teenage desire to break free was a necessary part of growing up for her. One of the benefits of getting older — at twenty-five she wasn't old, though she certainly felt more grounded than she had at eighteen or twenty-one — was gaining a greater appreciation for what she'd been lucky enough to experience.

She looked down at the phone in her hand and sighed. Her most vital tool was dead, its remaining power long gone. She'd managed a text to her dad before the battery hit zero, telling him the bus would pull into the town square a bit after noon. He'd texted back right away with a "Can't wait to see you!" and a smiley-face emoji. She'd chuckled at the smiley face, because she'd been the one to show him what emoji were, during her last visit home over the Fourth of July weekend. He'd scoffed at the cute little visual symbols, as he usually did with any new technology, but he'd allowed her to show him how to include them in his text messages. Now he used them all the time, with a fluency that surprised her.

The bus crested the ridge and Clara breathed in sharply at the breathtaking view of the valley below. It was a vista she never tired of. Below them, nestled amidst snow-covered fields and evergreen trees, lay the little town she called home. Even from this distance, she was able to make out the open square in the center of town. Further on was Heartsprings Lake, already frozen over. No doubt ice skaters were there right now, enjoying the bright winter day, blades flashing in the sunlight as they dashed across the smooth ice.

The bus wound closer to town and she felt her anticipation rising. The familiar sights warmed her. She'd grown up here — played in these yards, sledded in these meadows, fought fierce snowball fights on these streets with her friends and neighbors. As the bus passed the snow-covered town cemetery where her mom was buried, she felt the all-too-familiar pang of loss. Ten years had passed since her mom's death from breast cancer, and still the grief was raw and fresh. Her mom had been her inspiration — pushing her to live life to the fullest, to follow her dreams and not hold back. Clara felt comfort in knowing that, by moving to New York, she'd pursued her dreams with everything she had. She sometimes sensed her mom was with her, looking over her shoulder, proud of the young woman her daughter had become.

Everywhere she looked were reminders of the season. Houses decorated with strings of lights. Reindeer pulling sleighs on lawn after lawn. And, of course, snowmen. Heartsprings Valley loved snowmen — and snowwomen and snowkids. It seemed like the town had an army of snowpeople spreading cheer for the Christmas season.

And not only snowpeople — but also snow animals! The bus passed a house with a giant snow-bunny, its ears sticking straight up as it munched on a giant carrot.

The bus passed another house, and her eyes widened at the sight of —

A snow *hippo*?

She laughed out loud. Okay, sure. Probably the coldest hippo in the history of hippopotamuses, but why not?

The bus driver turned around. "Almost there, miss."

"Thank you." With a sigh of contentment, she started gathering her things.

A minute later, the bus turned a corner and pulled to the curb alongside the town square. She looked out the window at the familiar sights. Home sweet home!

The driver said, "Need any help? You know where to go from here?"

"I'm good, thanks." She picked up her bags and headed to the front. "I grew up here."

"Lucky you. Of all the towns on my route, Heart-springs Valley is my favorite."

"Mine, too. Hope you have a merry Christmas!"

"Merry Christmas to you, too."

She made her way down the steps and breathed in the crisp sharp air of home, blinking as her eyes adjusted to the bright mid-day light. In front of her, in the center of the square, stood the town's bandstand, which hosted concerts throughout the year. During the holiday season, townspeople gathered every evening to sing Christmas carols, the warmth and enthusiasm in their voices bringing joy to all who listened.

The four streets lining the square were filled with the small businesses that brought the town to life. She smiled as her eyes roved the square, pausing to take in the flower shop, cafe, and bookstore before landing on her dad's store, Cane Hardware. There, she knew, a certain someone was awaiting the arrival of his little girl who was all grown up now and living a fast-paced life in the big city.

Luggage in tow, she crossed the street and headed down the sidewalk, pausing as she passed Abby's Chocolate Heaven, one of her favorite shops. As usual, Abby had outdone herself with the window display, arranging a mouth-watering selection of tempting handmade treats. In the center of the display, Clara was pleased to see something new: a beautifully crafted gingerbread house of a lovely rustic cabin, decorated to perfection. On the gingerbread porch stood the gingerbread figures of a man, a woman, a big fluffy dog, and a regal-looking cat. A name card placed next to the house said, "Courtesy of Becca Shepherd."

Clara was tempted to go in, but she peered inside and saw that Abby was busy helping a customer at the counter. No, she'd swing by later to get a box (or two!) of delicious truffles and nougats to bring back to New York.

An idea came then: Perhaps her soon-to-arrive client could visit Abby's Chocolate Heaven, and maybe even help Abby whip up a batch of her home-made chocolates? The promotional possibilities would work two ways — Melody would get her small-town experience, and Abby would benefit from the publicity. Plus, Abby would be thrilled — she was a huge Broadway fan who made an annual pilgrimage to New York to "do the shows," as she put it.

Clara reached for her phone to leave a reminder note for herself, then remembered the darn thing was dead. It was then that she heard it: a rich, melodic voice — a voice with effortless stage presence, a voice that seemed to float, clear as crystal, through the crisp air:

"Yoooo-hoo! Clara dear, over here!"

CHAPTER 3

*E*ven without turning, Clara knew who was yoo-hooing her. That lovely voice, which delighted and charmed audiences nightly on the Broadway stage, was one she knew all too well.

Clara arranged her mouth into a smile, took a deep breath, and turned to find an enormous limousine parked alongside the square. Black and sleek, the limo seemed to go on forever, and was very out of place.

A face peered out from the rear window. It was a beautiful face, with high cheekbones, a perfect nose, unblemished skin, vivacious green eyes, and a wide, expressive mouth — all framed by a rich tumble of red hair.

The face belonged to Melody Connelly, winner of the Tony award for Best Actress in a Musical for her role as a plucky farm widow who charms a Duke in

London, Here I Come!. The play, a musical-comedy
smash, showcased Melody's impressive vocal skills
and dazzling stage presence, and had vaulted her to
worldwide fame. As one reviewer noted, "Ms.
Connelly's ability to charm an audience remains as
potent as ever, evoking laughs and tears in equal
measure for her portrayal of independent-minded
Sally, an impoverished widow thrown by fate into a
Duke's oh-so-willing arms."

It was a face that Clara had learned to become
wary of in the months since Melody had hired Nigel
to manage her press. Not because Melody was a bad
person — far from it. Most of the time, in fact, she
was charming and gracious, and always willing to
lend her talent for charitable causes. In quiet
moments, she'd even shown herself to be rather
sweet.

Rather, the trouble with Melody Connelly lay in
the fact that she was a diva in the best sense of the
word. She asked for the world and expected the
world, regardless of obstacles, and most of the time
she got what she asked for. No request was too
implausible, no idea too impractical, no flight of
fancy too grand or absurd to be made real.

Like the elephant. For Clara, it would always
come back to the elephant.

"Darling," Melody had said to Clara on that
pachyderm-filled day, shortly after Clara had started
working for her. The two of them were in a designer's

studio in the Fashion District where Melody was getting final fittings for her gown for the Central Park Gala, one of the most prestigious social events of the year. As the toast of Broadway, Melody knew that the world's eyes would be upon her on the red carpet. Which meant that, along with her excitement about attending, she was nervous about pulling off a media splash.

The star was standing in front of a bank of mirrors in the atelier, staring with approval at the gorgeous couture beaded silver gown she had just slipped into. The gown, a stunning update of a classic Chanel number from the 1930s, had taken the designer and his sewing team two weeks to stitch by hand.

Through the bank of mirrors, Melody looked at Clara and said, "I've just had the most marvelous little idea."

"Oh, really?" Clara said, steeling herself. In their short time working together, she'd quickly learned that Melody's "marvelous little ideas" usually meant lots of work — for Clara.

"Yes, darling. Just marvelous."

"I'm all ears," Clara said, glad her voice sounded upbeat. "That gown, by the way … I cannot tell you how stunning you look in it. It fits you to perfection."

"Thank you. But it's not enough."

"You mean, you want to try it with a different necklace or earrings?"

"Oh, no, not that," Melody said, turning back to the mirrors to admire the dazzling diamond necklace around her neck. "The necklace is perfect. What I mean is — walking in. It's just so passé. Everyone will be doing it."

"Doing what?"

"Walking."

"You mean," Clara said, not sure what Melody was getting at, "walking the red carpet?"

Melody clapped her hands together and laughed out loud, her gorgeous face alive with excitement.

"What if I don't?"

"Don't what?"

"Walk."

Clara paused, then said, "What would you do instead?"

"I could ride in."

"Ride in?"

"On an *elephant!* Wouldn't that be divine?"

The panic hit then. Surely her client realized how impossible that was?

Melody laughed. "Darling, I see by your face that you're positively flummoxed! That's just the response I want — from everyone! Such an incredible surprise. Won't it be just grand?"

"Melody," Clara said, recovering her composure. "The event is tomorrow. I don't think we can get an elephant."

"Nonsense," Melody said firmly. "Nigel was right

about you. You are a godsend. In our brief time together, I've seen you pull off all manner of miracles."

Clara slowly shook her head. "Not this time," she said, doing her best to remain calm. "There would be permits and planning, and trainers to hire, and the gala organizers would have to rebuild the stage to carry the extra weight, and we'd probably need extra security and insurance and...."

She trailed off when she saw the disappointment on her client's face. "Well, you know about these things, don't you?" the diva said quietly. "I'm sure you're right."

Clara felt it then — the pang of guilt at not living up to expectations. "I tell you what. Let me look into it. No promises. But I'll make some calls."

"Oh, would you, darling? Thank you, you're such a dear!" Good humor restored, Melody turned to the designer and gave him a dazzling smile. "Fernando, this dress is beyond perfect. I'm over the moon!"

In the end, there had been no elephant, of course. But not for lack of trying. Clara had spent the rest of that day and evening getting closer than she ever would have expected to achieving Melody's impossible dream before confirming that, indeed, renting an elephant for a high-profile red-carpet event in the heart of New York City required more than a day's notice. Fortunately, Melody had accepted that reality with good grace and walked the red carpet with elegance and enthusiasm.

Hopefully there would be no such elephantine requests in Heartsprings Valley. From her window in the back of the way-too-long limousine, Melody waved energetically at Clara. "Yoo-hoo!" she said again, her gorgeous voice effortlessly carrying on the crisp mid-day air. "I've arrived!"

CHAPTER 4

*F*or a long second, Clara wondered whether Heartsprings Valley would survive the coming whirlwind.

She set down her suitcase and made her way across the street to the limousine. "Melody, welcome to Heartsprings Valley!"

Melody laughed and pushed open the door, one long leg following the other as she stepped into the sunlight.

"Darling," Melody said, reaching down to give Clara a quick hug. "I'm so happy to see you."

"It's wonderful to see you, too," Clara said, not quite truthfully. She stepped back to admire Melody's cream cashmere sweater, soft brown leather pants and knee-high brown leather boots. Everything about the Broadway star looked effortlessly chic. "I love those boots."

"Oh, me, too," Melody said, looking down to admire them. "I hope they're appropriate."

"They're perfect. Don't you worry."

"Oh, but I am worried," Melody said, rather dramatically, aiming her dazzling green eyes at Clara. "I feel like such a fish."

"A fish?"

"Out of water. It's been so long since I've experienced the rough-and-tumble of the real world. I've been so cloistered, so cut off, from everything that's honest and true. Such is life on the stage."

Clara had learned, over the past three months, that Melody expected agreement from her audience. "I hear what you're saying."

Melody allowed her gaze to wander. "What a charming little town! So quaint. Oh, I almost forgot." She reached back into the limo and grabbed her phone. "We must record all the important moments, mustn't we?" She pressed the video button and aimed the camera at herself and said, "I made it, darlings! I'm so excited to be here, in Heartsprings Valley!"

She turned off the video, then turned toward Clara. "So, tell me everything!"

Clara almost responded with a "Huh?" but stopped herself just in time. A realization was dawning: Melody had no game plan. She'd driven up here on an impulse, with no idea (beyond filming herself with her phone) about what she was going to do.

Instead, she expected Clara to have a fully formed itinerary for every single moment of her small-town visit.

Clara willed her face to remain in neutral position. When she got back to New York, she and Nigel were going to have a long talk about the importance of communications and advance planning.

But that would be then. This was now. "What we're going to do," she said, with a focus on keeping her tone professional, her mind in overdrive as she improvised a plausible approach from scratch, "is immerse ourselves in the rhythms and pace of small-town life, beginning with a visit to Cane Hardware."

"*Cane* Hardware?" Melody asked, immediately discerning the connection.

"My dad's store," she said with a nod. "When we get there, I'll plug in my phone — no battery — so we can confirm your reservation at Heartsprings Valley Inn." She pointed to the limousine. "Is your luggage in here? And is the limo with you for your entire stay?"

Melody shook her head. "No, the driver has to return to New York after he drops off my bags."

Clara stifled the groan that desperately wanted to burst forth. No limo meant that Melody might also need a car. There were no rental car companies in Heartsprings Valley. Who was she going to persuade to lend Melody their car?

"Okay. The Inn is a few blocks away, so let's have

the driver go there and drop off your stuff while we go to my dad's store. Then we can walk to the Inn and get you settled in."

"Perfect," Melody said, her eyes lighting up with enthusiasm at the sight of all the Christmas decorations blanketing the town square. "Will you look at those adorable snowmen?"

"We're a very pro-snowman town," Clara said. She gave the driver directions to the Inn and asked if he would take in Melody's luggage. "Please tell Barbara and Stu — they're the innkeepers — that Clara Cane will be calling in a few minutes to explain." The driver nodded and headed off.

Clara turned to Melody. "Ready for your small-town Christmas experience?"

Melody held up her phone and said, with a giggle, "Lead the way!"

CHAPTER 5

The sidewalk was crammed with shoppers carrying bags bursting with gifts and holiday treats. Clara, suitcase trailing behind her, cleared a path through the crowd as Melody and her camera captured the scene.

"What you're doing with the camera is perfect," Clara ad-libbed more. "Whenever you see something you like, film it. When we cut the footage later, the handheld motion will help make everything feel spontaneous and real."

"Clara, I'm so excited. Such an adventure we're on!"

You have no idea, Clara thought.

When they reached her dad's store, Clara glanced at the window display and noted that it was in disarray. A ladder was poking up into the paneled ceiling, and the usual assortment of Christmas lights and decorations seemed to be pushed aside. Her dad was an excellent businessman, but a messy window display two days before Christmas was a definite no-no.

Mentally, she added another item to her holiday to-do list: Fix whatever was going on with the window display.

She turned to Melody. "Here we are!"

Together, they stepped inside. Immediately, Clara felt like she had traveled back in time. She'd grown up in this store — played in the aisles as a child, worked behind the cash register as a teenager, helped reorganize the stockroom during breaks from college. The familiar smells washed over her — the scent of pine needles sprinkled over the floor, carried in from the Christmas trees on sale in the lot out back. The usual hints of garden soil and cut lumber. A waft of fresh paint, probably from a customer who'd opened a can for a color test.

And the bustle! Shoppers were everywhere — in the aisles, arriving and leaving, waiting in line to pay for their purchases. The tall shelves, which ran all the way to the ceiling, were, as always, laden with all manner of goods.

As she led Melody deeper inside, she realized something was missing. She wasn't feeling the usual welcome blast of heat. The temperature in the store wasn't much different from the cold winter air outside. She frowned, her mind zeroing in on that when —

"Clara!" a familiar voice said.

She turned and found herself enveloped in a big warm welcome hug — by her dad. He picked her up in his strong arms and swirled her around, just like he did when she was little.

"Dad!" she said happily. "Merry Christmas!"

"So glad you're here," he said in his usual booming voice, then set her down and took a step back. "You're a sight for sore eyes."

She grinned. He was looking like his rough-and-tumble self, dressed (as usual) in blue coveralls and a blue Cane Hardware sweatshirt, his tool belt (as always) wrapped around his waist. His grey eyes were alive with happiness at seeing her, his bald pate gleaming in the overhead light, a huge grin on his broad friendly face.

"How was your trip?" he asked.

"Fine. I'm so glad to be here. Everything here's looking good. Except I noticed —"

Oh, gosh — she'd nearly forgotten!

"Dad," she said, with a wave of her hand, "I'd like to introduce you to someone."

Her dad followed her hand and, for the first time, noticed Melody.

"Dad, this is Melody Connelly."

Melody stood there expectantly, waiting for the usual response from her adoring public: delighted recognition followed by gushing adulation.

Her dad stuck out his hand. "Pleased to meet you, Melody. Are you a friend of Clara's?"

With a start, Clara realized her dad didn't know who Melody was.

Melody realized the same — even big stars occasionally went unrecognized, after all — and adjusted instantly. "Pleased to meet you, too." She took his hands in both of hers. "I'm so very glad to be here in Heartsprings Valley. Clara has told me such wonderful things about her hometown."

"Glad to hear."

"Dad," Clara said, "I work with Melody in New York. She's an amazing actress and singer — she won a Tony award on Broadway this year — and Nigel and I help manage her media."

"Clara is too kind," Melody said. "She is a delight to work with. I adore her."

"We're glad to have you, Melody," her dad said. "Welcome to Heartsprings Valley." He turned to Clara with a question in his eyes.

Clara knew exactly what he was about to ask, so she jumped right in. "Melody is spending a few days here in preparation for a TV show."

"Is that so?" her dad said, sounding impressed.

"She'll be staying at the Inn." She held up her

phone. "I need to talk to Barbara and Stu, but my phone's dead and I need to charge it."

"Behind the counter."

"Thanks," she said, then turned to Melody. "Tell Dad more about what you're after — he might have ideas for us."

CHAPTER 6

*C*lara reached into her travel bag, pulled out her charger, and stepped to the counter. The cashier, a woman whom Clara recognized by sight but whose name she was blanking on, turned around as Clara slipped behind her and gave her a smile.

"Clara," the woman said. "So good to see you."

"Thank you," Clara replied, wracking her brain to remember the woman's name. "It's good to see you, too."

The woman was in her mid-forties, with shoulder-length brown hair pulled back into a ponytail and a warm, open face. She was dressed in sneakers, jeans, and a red Cane Hardware sweatshirt. "Your father has been talking about you nonstop the past few weeks. He's so excited you're here for Christmas."

"I'm glad to be here, too." The name came to her

then: *Peggy.* Her dad had mentioned her in a recent phone call. If Clara was remembering right, Peggy was the store's new assistant manager.

Clara found the electrical outlet and plugged in her phone. "Dad looks like he's doing well."

"Oh, he is," Peggy replied.

Clara glanced down the aisle to where her dad was gabbing and laughing with her client. That was the thing about her dad — he was good with people. Much better than she was. Not that she was bad at it — she just had to work at it more.

"How's the store doing?" Clara said as she glanced at her phone. The charging had begun. Just a bit longer and she'd have enough juice to call the Inn.

"Oh, the usual amounts of crazy. Busiest time of year and all. And now with the heater going kaput...."

"The heater's out? I noticed it was chilly when I walked in."

"It gave out last night. I called my nephew — he's a contractor. He's finishing a job today and can squeeze us in. He'll be by any minute."

"Good," Clara said, her mind half-focused on the phone. "Do you happen to know the number for the Inn?"

Peggy pulled out the Heartsprings Valley phone book from behind the counter. "Here you go."

"Thanks." Clara quickly found the listing and

punched in the numbers. After two rings, someone picked up.

"Heartsprings Valley Inn," a female voice said. "How may I help you?"

"Barbara, is that you?"

"Clara, is that you?"

"It sure is!"

"Welcome back, and merry Christmas!" Barbara said.

Clara smiled. Barbara and her husband Stu were old friends of her parents. They'd moved to Heartsprings Valley twenty years back to buy the Inn and, after lovingly restoring it, had turned it into a gorgeous bed-and-breakfast. When her mom had gotten sick, Barbara and Stu had been rocks of support and friendship.

"Thank you so much," Clara said. "I think you can guess why I'm calling."

"When that big limousine pulled up, I said to Stu, 'Now who can that be?'" Barbara said with a hearty laugh. "And when the driver said it was Melody Connelly...."

"Is it okay for her to stay with you for a few days? Do you have room at the Inn?"

"You're in luck. We can put her in the Harvest Room."

"Thank you so much! I really appreciate it."

"Let me guess — she's one of your clients at that big fancy job of yours down in New York?"

"You got it."

"I bet there's a story there."

Clara smiled. "Isn't there always?"

Barbara laughed. "Whenever you're ready, bring her here. I saw her on TV a few weeks ago, singing that big song of hers. I'm looking forward to meeting her."

"We'll be by soon. Thank you so much!"

"See you soon!"

She placed her phone back on the counter and reviewed her ever-growing to-do list. At least she'd found Melody a place to sleep. She still had to track down a way for her client to get around town. And devise an itinerary of hometown happenings that would satisfy the Broadway star's unformed yet undoubtedly extravagant imaginings about what she might be doing while here....

She heard Melody laugh, her stage voice floating through the store, and looked over to see her dad and her client carrying on like they'd known each other forever.

"Is that who I think it is?" Peggy said.

"If you're wondering if that's Melody Connelly, then yes, it is."

"What is she doing here?"

Beats me, Clara almost blurted out. Instead she said, "She's visiting in preparation for a television show."

"What kind of preparation does she need?"

Clara shifted her attention to Peggy. Her dad's new assistant manager was asking an excellent question. She was in the presence of a fellow problem-solver.

"Experience, mostly," Clara said. "She's been in the fame bubble for the past two years, with barely a moment out of it."

Peggy nodded. "That must be exciting but also very demanding. Maybe she just needs to recharge."

"Maybe," Clara said. "I'm hoping for a few quiet days of recharging myself. Peace and quiet — that's all I want for Christmas."

Peggy chuckled. "Sign me up for that."

"I better go see what those two are laughing about."

"Anything I can help with," Peggy said, "let me know."

"Thanks."

Clara walked back to her dad and Melody.

"Darling," Melody said, "your father is full of marvelous ideas. I hope we can fit them in."

"We can try," Clara said cautiously. "What kind of ideas?"

"Well," her dad said. "We've got the Christmas Eve concert in the town square tomorrow night. I know they'd love for Melody to take part."

Clara grinned. "Great idea, Dad." And it was — arranging it would be a snap, and the visuals would be perfect.

"Your other idea sounds so divine," Melody said. "Can I tell her?"

"Please," her dad said with a grin.

"Your dad tells me that your town's annual Christmas cookie contest is tomorrow afternoon. And this year's theme is 'It Takes Two.'"

Clara frowned. She wasn't sure where Melody and her dad were going with this. She knew about Heartsprings Valley's annual Christmas cookie contest, of course, though she'd never entered — her mom had been the expert baker in the family, not her. But she saw from the expectant looks on their faces that they had something up their proverbial sleeves.

"Your dad hasn't told you this yet," Melody said with a conspiratorial glance at her dad, "but he's entered you in this year's contest."

"What?" Clara said, her eyes widening in alarm. "No, I couldn't. I wouldn't know what to bake."

"That's not what your dad says. He says you're a wizard in the kitchen — just like your mom was."

"Dad," Clara said, turning toward him.

"You and Peggy are going to do great," her dad said.

"Wait," Clara said, blinking in confusion. "Me and Peggy? What do you mean?"

"Since this year's contest is for pairs or partners — 'It Takes Two' — I thought the contest would be a great way for you and Peggy to get to know each other better."

Melody jumped in. "And your dad thinks I could be one of the judges!" She clasped her hands together. "Doesn't that sound divine?"

Divine for you, Clara thought, even as a more pressing thought swirled through her head: What was going on here? She was missing something. Her dad didn't usually act like this. Christmas cookie contests weren't on his radar. And why did he want her to get to know Peggy better?

"Dad," she said again. "You know I haven't been able to spend much time in the kitchen lately...."

"You're a natural," he said. "You can do this in your sleep."

Sleep — very funny. At this rate, was she ever going to get any?

But first things first. She turned to her client. "Melody, I love the idea of you being a judge for the cookie contest. And the concert on Christmas Eve sounds perfect."

She turned to her dad. "As for me entering the cookie contest, we'll see."

Her dad knew that tone, and knew it meant she was in no mood for a debate. He turned to Melody. "Melody, I have to get back to work — it's our busiest time of the year and I have a million things to do. Pleasure meeting you."

"A pleasure meeting you!" Melody said.

He turned back to Clara. "How about you head

home, freshen up, and come back when you're ready?"

"Sounds good. I'll do that after I get Melody settled at the Inn."

"Great." As he turned toward the storeroom, his attention was caught by something up front.

"Ah, good," he said. "The contractor's here. Just in time."

Clara turned and stopped breathing. A young man had just stepped into the store. He was wearing a mackinaw jacket, blue jeans, and brown work boots. At the counter, Peggy saw him and reached over to give him a hug.

A jolt of recognition tore through Clara, her heart thumping like a jackhammer. She felt the blood drain from her face.

Oh my — her face. What did her face look like? A plain, bare mess — that was what it looked like. And her hair — a big, curly mess. And her sweatshirt — she might as well be wearing a formless bag!

Of all the contractors who could have walked into her dad's store, why did it have to be him? Why did it have to be —

Luke Matthews?

CHAPTER 7

*S*he was thirteen again, or maybe fourteen — heck, any of her teen years would do. She was the shy girl again, the girl with the big glasses and silver braces, arms loaded with books, body full of awkward changes, head full of fears and anxieties.

She was back in the stands at her high school's football games. Or in the hallway at school, fumbling with her locker. Or walking home from school, watching a car full of older teenagers cruise by. Or in her dad's hardware store, manning the cash register.

She was in any of the thousand places he was. Occupying the same physical space but a million miles away. Gazing upon her hopeless teenage crush from an impossible distance. Pining away for a boy who was a huge three years older than her. The star quarterback of the Heartsprings Valley Panthers. The cutest boy in school, the most popular, the most athletic.

He never noticed her, of course, not really. Why would he? Why would a senior pay attention to a ninth-grader? Especially a ninth-grader with a mouth full of metal and a head full of shyness and insecurity?

Gah. What was Luke Matthews doing here now? He'd joined the Army after high school — was he out now? Was he back home now?

He was still as handsome as ever. The intervening decade had been good to him. If anything, he looked better than he had in high school. He'd filled out a bit, matured a bit. His sandy-blond hair was cut close, his blue eyes clear and bright, his stance upright. He'd kept in shape. Instinctively, her eyes went to his left hand and saw, with a jolt, that the third finger was bare.

Gah! Why was she looking at his left hand? What was wrong with her?

Maybe she could slip out the back — grab Melody and make a quick escape. And then hide under her bed until Christmas was over.

"Luke, glad you're here," she heard her dad say as he walked to the counter to greet her impossible crush.

"Happy to help out, Mr. Cane," Luke said. His voice sounded good — clear and direct and straight-ahead.

Her dad grinned. "None of this 'Mr. Cane' nonsense, young man. Call me Ted."

"Okay, Ted," Luke said with the same big wide grin that had gotten the butterflies fluttering in her stomach all those years ago. "I hear your heater needs attention."

Clara began formulating her exit plan. If she grabbed Melody by the arm and quietly led her out the back, she could avoid Luke laying eyes on her in her current "I-don't-care-what-I-look-like" state.

But then her dad did the unthinkable. To her horror, he gestured toward her. "Luke, do you remember my daughter Clara?"

Gah! There was no escape now.

Luke's blue eyes turned toward her with interest. His brow furrowed.

"She was a few years behind you in school," her dad added as he led Luke closer.

"Ah," Luke said, his face clearing. He gave her a friendly grin. Had he remembered her? He extended his hand. "You had braces and glasses back then, right?"

"Right," Clara managed to croak out, just barely. She realized his hand was waiting there for her, so she reached out and —

Bam! Electricity shot through her as their hands touched.

Luke blinked — he'd felt it, too. His blue eyes widened.

Half of her wanted to pull away in shock and embarrassment, but the other half of her was firmly opposed to any such course. His hand was larger than hers. It seemed to fit around hers perfectly. It was a strong hand, a bit rough. And it was warm. Very warm.

"Look at you — all grown up," he said, surprise in his tone. He opened his mouth to say more, then stopped, as if frozen.

They both realized in the same instant that their handshake was going on too long.

Clara withdrew. "It's been a long time," she said, her voice steadier than she had any right to expect. "Since high school. I don't think I've seen you since you joined the Army."

He nodded. "I got out about a year ago."

Peggy joined them. "Luke's working with his dad now in the family contracting business." She gave him an affectionate smile. "We sure are happy to have him back."

Luke wrapped an arm around her and pulled her in for a hug. "Aunt Peggy's a sweetheart."

Peggy flushed with pleasure. "He's such a help to his dad."

Luke shrugged modestly and returned his attention to Clara. Once again, she felt the pull of those startlingly clear eyes. "I haven't seen you around town," he said, his gaze shifting to the suitcase next to her. "Here for a visit?"

"I live in New York."

"Ah." Was she imagining things or did she sense a lessening of energy — even a hint of disappointment?

Feeling an urge to switch attention away from herself, she asked, "You happy to be back in Heartsprings Valley?"

"Real happy." He glanced at his Aunt Peggy. "I didn't realize until I got back how much I'd missed this place."

His words cut right through her. *I miss this place, too,* she almost said.

Her dad, who had been silently watching their awkward exchange, noticed a customer with a question. "Excuse me," he said. "Duty calls."

As her dad stepped away, Clara noticed Luke's attention shift — to the dazzling Broadway star next to her. He blinked and his mouth opened.

"Do I know you?" he said with a puzzled frown.

Melody smiled. "We haven't met. Melody Connelly. I'm a singer and actor."

"Luke," Peggy said, "you know her song, 'Two Is the Best Number.'"

Recognition lit up his face. "You're in that play...."

"Yes," Melody said with a pleased laugh.

Peggy said to Melody, "I'm Peggy, by the way. A big fan. Pleased to meet you."

"Pleased to meet you, too."

Luke said to Melody, "What are you doing up *here*?"

Melody laughed again — a beautiful laugh, just like everything else about her — and slipped an arm through Clara's. "I'm here in Heartsprings Valley to experience everything that can be experienced in a small New England town at Christmas. With Clara's help, of course."

"I work with Melody," Clara added. "I help with her media. She's considering a move into TV."

"A TV show?" Luke said. "What kind?"

Clara glanced up at Melody, not sure what else her client was willing to reveal.

Melody said, "I might be hosting a show on the Gourmet TV channel. The show explores great American cooking. I'll be traveling across the country to meet wonderful chefs — many of them in small towns like this one."

"So your visit up here is kind of a test run?"

"I like how you put that," she said with a dazzling smile. "And your name is ... Luke?"

He started as he realized he hadn't properly introduced herself. "Luke Matthews," he said, extending his hand. "Pleased to meet you."

Clara's stomach clenched as she watched Luke's hand grip Melody's. Before she even knew what she was doing, she said brightly, "Melody, we need to get you settled into your room at the Inn."

"Ah," Melody said. She released Luke's hand

— with reluctance, perhaps, or was Clara imagining that? — and turned her gaze toward Clara. "We're getting in the way here, aren't we? If I heard right, there's a heater that needs fixing?"

"That's right," Clara said, then turned to Luke. "Great seeing you again after all these years."

"Same here," he said, his eyes holding hers.

"Clara," Peggy said, glancing quickly at Luke and then back at her, "I know you have a lot on your plate, but your dad and I were wondering if you could swing by later this afternoon, if you're not too busy, of course. What with the holiday crush, I was hoping you might be able to help with the window display up front. When the heater went out, we had to move stuff around, and we haven't had even a second today to fix it back up."

"Of course," Clara said, pleased that Peggy had asked. It was nice knowing that Peggy was on the same page as her about the importance of the display.

"Luke," Peggy said, "let's get you to that heater."

"Absolutely," Luke said. "Good to see you again after all these years, Clara. And nice meeting you, Melody."

The two of them watched Peggy lead him away, toward the back of the store.

Melody pivoted toward Clara, a small smile on her face. "You knew him back in high school?"

"Kind of," Clara said, cursing inwardly as she felt blood rush to her face.

"He's cute," Melody said, then giggled. "And as nice-looking from the back as the front."

Clara had noted the very same thing, but she was *not* going to get into a discussion about Luke Matthews' attractiveness. Not with anyone, and certainly not with her glamorous client!

Melody, apparently discerning from Clara's face that Luke was not a comfortable topic of conversation, decided to take pity. "So, about that room at the Inn?"

"Yes," Clara said with relief. "The Inn is just a short walk. I can show you some of the town on the way."

"Lead the way, Clara Cane," Melody said, her gorgeous green eyes twinkling. "Lead the way!"

CHAPTER 8

*O*utside in the town square, the winter sun was still blindingly bright. Melody, phone in hand, was enthusiastically filming every single snowman they passed. "Will you look at that one?" she said, zooming in on a snow-reindeer with a bright red nose. "So adorable!"

Clara managed to keep a smile on her face, but inside she was deep in anxiety mode. Oh, what a day. And it was barely past lunchtime! Her to-do list kept getting longer. Clearly, her heartfelt wish for a relaxing Christmas was doomed to be nothing but a hopeless fantasy.

Which was really too bad. She needed a few moments of quiet right now — so many things for her to chew on. So many little things that weren't quite lining up.

Starting with her client. Why was Melody here,

really? Preparing for a TV show was a perfectly valid reason to visit a small town like Heartsprings Valley. But right now, two days before Christmas? Surely her client had plans for the holiday?

Or ... maybe not? She realized she didn't know Melody as well as she could. In certain ways, she understood her quite well — how she managed her professional life, for example. But in other respects, what did she know, really? Over the past three months, had Melody mentioned her family even once?

There was, of course, one person she had mentioned an awful lot: her new beau, the famous action-movie star Derek Davies. Clara had heard all about how he and Melody met ("on a yacht at Cannes — utterly charming!"), how he wooed her ("he swept me away for a lovely weekend in Bermuda — so divine!"), how much he supported her ("red roses for my two-hundredth performance — so thoughtful!"), and more. For the past three months, Clara had been subjected to a nearly nonstop stream of "Derek this, Derek that."

Though not today, at least not yet. Her client hadn't said anything yet about her charming, divine, thoughtful beau. Was there a reason for that?

Clara's winter boots crunched in the light dusting of snow covering the path. They were in the center of the town square now, approaching the bandstand used for concerts and theatrical performances throughout the year. On Christmas Eve, the bandstand would host the annual Heartsprings Valley Christmas concert. She made a mental note to call the choir's director, Bert Winters, to ask if Melody could join in. Bert would be thrilled, she knew — he loved welcoming strangers to town.

"And here," Clara said, her breath floating into the crisp air, "is where the Christmas Eve concert takes place."

"Oh, how lovely," Melody said, her eyes sweeping the small stage. "What's the sound system like?"

"I'll ask the choir director. His name is Bert, by the way. He'll be so excited to meet you."

Melody gave a happy sigh. "This town is so beautiful. Truly, an undiscovered gem."

"I'm glad you like it."

"And your father is so friendly and welcoming."

"He's the best."

"And his — I take it she's his girlfriend, Peggy? — seems very nice, too."

"Girlfriend?" Clara said, stopping short. They'd reached the far side of the square and were about to cross the street. Why would Melody think her dad was dating Peggy? "No, they're not dating. Peggy's the assistant manager at the store."

"Ah," Melody said. "Sorry. Misinterpreting signals — I do it all the time. Well, as I was saying, she seems very nice. Just like everyone else in this town."

After looking both ways for traffic, Clara led

Melody across the street to the sidewalk in front of the Tattered Page, the town's treasured independent bookstore. Shoppers bustled past them, looking for the perfect Christmas gift for their loved ones.

She paused in front of the bookstore, her sleep-deprived brain trying to prioritize and categorize the jumble of ideas racing through her head. She was usually quite good at organizing herself and others — she had a natural affinity for it. So why was her brain refusing to cooperate right now?

Even with the sun at its highest point in the sky, the air was too crisp for dilly-dallying — and neither she nor Melody was bundled up enough to remain outside for long. Next to her, Melody peered through the window display. "I love bookstores. Before the show, before life became a nonstop blur, I used to haunt the bookstores in New York."

Clara's eyebrows rose as she digested that nugget. The Melody Connelly she knew wasn't much of a reader. "I didn't know you liked books."

"There's always one on my night stand," her client replied. "Nowadays, bed is the only place I can snuggle in with a good read. Can we go in?"

The question helped Clara figure out her plan of attack for the afternoon. "Let's go to the Inn first and get you settled. Then, later today, I can introduce you to some of the businesses on the square, including the bookstore, and get your small-town expedition under way."

"That sounds wonderful. It would be nice to freshen up."

They set out for the Inn, two blocks off the square, with Clara providing a running commentary as they walked. "Heartsprings Valley was founded after the Revolutionary War by a businessman named Jedediah Heartsprings. Jedediah started a lumber mill here, and the town sprang up around it. His descendants lived on in Heartsprings Valley for more than two hundred years."

They passed a beautiful Victorian mansion, its turrets and spires dusted with snow. "This mansion is where the last member of the Heartsprings clan lived. Her name was Minerva Heartsprings. I remember her from when I was a kid. In the summer, she'd sit on the porch in her favorite rocker, passing the time of day with everyone who walked by. She was always so nice to me. She told wonderful stories about the old days."

Melody looked at the porch and sighed. "Such history. What a wonderful sense of place you have here."

"Auntie Minerva — that's what we all called her — was so supportive of me and my dad after my mom died."

"You've mentioned your mom before. She died ... a decade ago?"

Clara nodded. "Coming up on ten years now."

"I'm so sorry. I can only imagine how difficult that was for you and your dad."

"Harder than anything I've ever experienced." A pang of grief, never far from the surface, threatened to burst forth, but Clara managed to keep it at bay.

Melody seemed to be about to say something — maybe about her own family? — before changing her mind and switching gears. "Is Auntie Minerva still around?"

Clara shook her head. "She died a few years ago, at the age of 102, active and alert right up till the end."

"My goodness," Melody said. "Such a long life!"

"The Heartsprings mansion is now a veterinary clinic — an excellent one, I'm told."

Shoes crunching lightly on the salted sidewalk, they moved past the mansion toward another large home at the end of the same block. It was a grand residence in the Queen Anne style, painted pale blue with white trim, featuring a lovely wide porch that started at the front door and wrapped around the side of the house. Two stories above the porch, an intricate Dutch gable roof rose next to a circular tower topped with a weather vane shaped like a rooster, moving gently in the breeze. Despite the intricacy of its design, the house exuded an air of calm and welcome. The front lawn, covered with a light blanket of snow, sported a welcoming snow-man, his arms spread in greeting. Next to him, a sign between two posts read, "Heartsprings Valley Inn."

Irresistibly, Clara felt herself drawn closer, and sensed Melody was under the same spell.

"Oh, Clara," Melody breathed. "How divine."

They made their way up the stone path and onto the front porch. An oversize Christmas wreath decorated the heavy oak door. Nestled inside the wreath was a hand-written sign: "Come on in!"

With a rush of anticipation, Clara pushed open the heavy front door and stepped into the warmth of the Inn's front parlor. Immediately, the delightful aroma of freshly baked chocolate cookies greeted her, along with a welcome embrace of heat.

Melody gasped with pleasure. "How charming." Indeed, the Inn's beautifully restored interior — wide-plank honey-brown hardwood floors, cream-colored plaster walls, and crisp white ceilings — set the stage for a delightful selection of furnishings and accessories. In the parlor, where they stood, Clara's eyes roved from the solid antique sideboard up to the oil painting on the wall above it. The painting showed Heartsprings Valley's town square at dawn on a winter morning, a gentle rendering that faith-fully captured the town's spirit. Her eyes wandered up further to the ornate wrought-iron chandelier, draped with crystals that sparkled in the reflected sunlight.

From where they stood in the front parlor, they

could see into the home's living room, furnished with an eclectic mix of sofas and side chairs arranged for conversation and relaxation. Reminders of the season were everywhere: a statue of Santa Claus on a sideboard, a jar of tempting candy canes on a coffee table, and, in a corner of the room, a huge Christmas tree adorned with all manner of decorations, with lights twinkling merrily and a silver star at the top that nearly brushed the high ceiling.

Clara's eyes turned from the living room to something even more beautiful: the meticulously restored staircase that rose from the entry foyer to the Inn's second and third floors. Clara knew the staircase well — restoring it to its original glory had been a labor of love for Barbara and Stu, and for her parents, too, who had pitched in to help them bring it back to life. She'd been eight years old the summer they tackled the staircase. Clara had been eager to help out, but her parents had explained that the restoration was for grownups. "You can come to Barbara's house with us," her mother had told her, "but only if you promise to stay in the kitchen and read and draw." After she promised to do so, they set her up in the kitchen at a small dining table overflowing with books and crayons and drawing paper. "Remember," her dad said. "You stay back here." But she'd been a curious and willful child — she couldn't help herself, really— so it was perhaps no surprise that, after happily drawing a picture of a beautiful chestnut horse, she noticed the smell of fresh paint wafting from the front parlor and decided to investigate. As she passed through the kitchen, she spied a plate of freshly baked cookies on the counter, and inspiration hit: If she had a reason for going in there, maybe her parents would let her stay?

Seconds later, the plate of cookies in her little hands and a smile on her face, she stepped into the front parlor. "I brought you cookies," she announced to her parents, who were kneeling on different sections of the staircase, paint brushes in hand, laughing at something that had escaped her eight-year-old ears. "Thank you, honey," her dad replied, "but I can't really have one right now. Why don't you take the plate back to the kitchen and sit back down with your drawings and books? I'll take a break in a minute and join you."

Not easily deterred, Clara turned to her mother. "What are you and Daddy talking about, Mommy?" she asked, eager to be part of the conversation. Her mother gave her a warm smile. "Just grownup stuff, dear. Those cookies look wonderful, but do as Dad says and take them back to the kitchen." To which Clara had replied, "But I'm becoming a grownup, right?" Her mother had given her a long, loving, wistful look. "Oh, darling. All too soon, before you and I know it, you will be. Time goes by so fast."

Clara blinked away a welling of tears. Her mother was right about that — time seemed to go by so fast.

No matter where she turned in this town, it seemed her mother was there. Back in high school, when her grief was raw and fresh and bottomless and seemingly without end, the memories had brought nothing but pain. But now ... she realized how glad she was to have those memories. How wonderful it was to be able to remember her mom on these stairs, laughing with her dad.

She heard the familiar sound of hinges creaking on the Inn's swinging kitchen door, and turned toward a beloved figure in a baking apron rushing toward her.

"Clara!" Barbara said as she pulled Clara in for a hearty hug. "Welcome home!"

CHAPTER 9

*C*lara gasped as Barbara's squeeze nearly took her breath away. "So good to see you," she said, barely able to get out the words. That was the thing about Barbara — she didn't hold back, not ever. If she felt it, she showed it. If she thought it, she said it. Taller and more sturdily built than Clara, with short graying brown hair, lively brown eyes, and a wide mouth that grinned at a second's notice, she never seemed to stop moving — a good trait to have as an innkeeper. Today she was dressed in a white apron over a red-and-white holiday-themed sweater, along with blue jeans and sneakers. Barbara loved everything about the Inn, but the kitchen was her preferred domain.

"Do I smell your famous chocolate-chip cookies?" Clara asked with a smile, still enveloped in Barbara's warm embrace.

Barbara laughed. "Fresh out of the oven." She set Clara free, then turned to Melody and extended her hand. "We are so glad to have you here, Ms. Connelly. What a pleasure to have such a big star staying at the Inn."

"Thank you. Everything here is so lovely," Melody said, returning the handshake.

"It's a lot of work, but Stu and I — Stu's my husband, out on errands right now — we love it."

Clara said to Melody, "I've known Barbara and Stu since I was a kid."

"She used to be such a little thing," Barbara said. "Shy, big glasses, nose always in a book."

Melody grinned. "I would hardly describe her as shy now."

"I hope not, not with that busy job of hers in New York." She gave Clara a quick but thorough inspection. "You're looking too skinny, dear. We'll have to do something about that."

"I'm fine," Clara protested. "Just a bit tired is all. A few days of rest and I'll be good as new."

"You, rest? Ha! This girl," Barbara said, turning to face Melody, "works nonstop. Can't help herself. Always adding stuff to her to-do lists. Been that way her whole life."

"Barbara...."

"Now, now, dear. I know you — never forget that." She said it with a tenderness that caused Clara to blink with surprise. Barbara was right — she really did know her, in a way that few in New York really did.

Clara suppressed another tearful impulse and said, with a shrug and a rueful smile, "Okay, you're right. I'm a list-maker. There, I admitted it. So we might as well tackle the first item on my list: getting Melody checked in."

Barbara smiled and turned back to Melody. "Ms. Connelly—"

"Please, call me Melody."

"Melody, we have you in the Harvest Room, one flight up. Stu brought up your luggage earlier." She led them up the beautiful stairs to the second floor, which had four guest suites, and pushed open an oak door decorated with a painting of a pumpkin surrounded by autumn leaves. Clara and Melody followed her in.

"Oh, Barbara," Melody said, "how lovely." The room was graciously proportioned, with a king-size bed facing beautiful bay windows. A two-seat sofa tucked near the windows looked temptingly comfortable, its creamy white cushions begging for someone to curl in with a good book. The room's decor breathed autumn, from the warm honey-brown walls to the auburns, ochres, and yellows in the furnishings and accessories. On the bed, the crisp white sheets and pillows were covered with a gorgeous autumnal quilt — a handmade treasure with a burgundy-red base and an explosion of fall leaves.

While Barbara pointed out the room's various features to Melody, Clara stepped across the room and peeked into the bathroom. Like the rest of the suite, it was luxuriously and thoughtfully updated. The palette was brighter and more on the neutral side, with walls a pale gray, a modern walk-in shower with gray stone tiles, and a standalone claw-foot bathtub on a black-and-white checkerboard tile floor. Burgundy towels stacked in a rack next to a refinished white pedestal sink completed the look.

Melody peeked in over Clara's shoulder. "Beautiful," she said, turning back toward Barbara. "So charming, just like everything else about this Inn and this town."

"How long will you be staying, Melody?" Barbara asked.

A very good question. Clara looked toward her client and waited for the answer.

Melody blinked and, after a short pause, said, "I have to be back in New York by the evening of Christmas Day. I recently started dating someone and … he's whisking me away for a skiing holiday in Switzerland."

Inwardly, Clara breathed a sigh of relief, happy that Melody had plans.

Barbara gave her a mischievous smile. "Does that someone go by the name of Derek Davies?"

Melody blushed. "You've heard?"

"We may live in a small town, but we do get news

from the outside world. I love Derek Davies — he's so good in those movies of his. When I heard the two of you were dating, I said to Stu, 'Now don't they look good together? And they're both so talented.'"

"That's very sweet."

"We'll do everything we can to make your visit here as comfortable and enjoyable as possible."

Clara jumped in. "Okay, here's our plan of attack."

"See?" Barbara said. "Girl can't help herself."

Melody laughed, but Clara ignored them both and continued on. "I'm going to go home and freshen up and make a few calls to confirm some of the stuff we've lined up for Melody."

"Lined up for Melody?" Barbara asked.

"She's here to experience life in a small town as preparation for a new cooking show about great American cuisine."

"Oh, that sounds wonderful."

"One of the calls is to Bert Winters, to see about Melody taking part in the Christmas Eve concert in the town square."

"Perfect."

"And I was thinking I could arrange for Melody to spend some time with Abby at the chocolate shop."

"Abby will love that," Barbara said. "What else do you have planned?"

"A tour of the shops in the town square, of course. And for the rest, we'll play it by ear."

"Clara, darling, you're forgetting something," Melody said with a twinkle in her eye.

"What's that?"

Melody turned to Barbara. "Clara's father had a marvelous idea. He suggested that perhaps I could be one of the judges for the Heartsprings Valley Christmas Cookie Contest."

Barbara's eyes lit up. "I love that idea! And you know what, you've come to the right place."

"What do you mean?" Clara asked.

"I'm one of the judges this year. I'll give the other judges a call — I'm sure they'll be thrilled to have you join us."

"Oh, that's terrific," Melody said.

"Thank you, Barbara," Clara added. "One less item on my to-do list."

"Good," Melody said, "because it sounds like you've forgotten one more thing."

Barbara said, "What's that?"

"Clara's dad has entered her in this year's cookie contest."

"Is that so?" Barbara said, turning to Clara. "Who are you entering with? You know this year's theme is 'It Takes Two.'"

"Clara's father entered Clara and Peggy, from the hardware store."

"Ah," Barbara said with a knowing nod. "Good."

"I don't know why he did that," Clara said. "I haven't baked in forever."

Barbara looked at her fondly. "Oh, you'll be fine. You're a natural in the kitchen, just like your mom." She turned to Melody and said briskly, "We'll get out of your way and let you unpack and freshen up. I'll be downstairs in the kitchen. Come down and chat when you're ready — I love getting to know our guests. If you need anything" — she pointed to the phone on the nightstand next to the bed — "press zero."

"Thank you so much," Melody said.

"I'll call in about an hour," Clara said to her client.

"Thank you both!"

Barbara ushered Clara out the door and gently shut it behind her, then led Clara down the stairs to the foyer.

"It's so good to see you, dear," Barbara said.

"I'm glad to be home," Clara replied.

"Stu and I will take good care of her. Don't you worry."

"Thank you."

"From the looks of it, we're going to have to take care of you as well."

"Barbara...."

"You look bone-tired, my dear."

"I'm fine."

"If you say so," Barbara said, looking steadily into Clara's eyes. "Go home. Relax. Freshen up. We'll get you sorted out. Now go."

CHAPTER 10

Twenty minutes later, Clara let out a huge sigh as the tension of the day began to seep away. She was back in her childhood home, a short two-block walk from the Inn. Back in the bedroom she'd grown up in, lying on her twin bed, staring at walls decorated with paintings and posters and post-it notes that she'd barely touched since she'd left for college more than seven years earlier.

The room was quiet — blessedly so. She needed this moment of respite. She closed her eyes and took a deep breath, then exhaled. After a pause, she breathed in and out again, feeling herself settle back into her preferred zone.

She'd always been a born organizer. Setting her mind to a task — from the simplest all the way up to the most complex — had always felt so right.

Keeping herself busy and focused had always brought her so much satisfaction, especially when the task was about helping someone else.

Opening her eyes, she surveyed the familiar surroundings. She and her dad hadn't changed a thing. The room was a museum, an artifact of her high-school years, a window into the girl she once was. Her gaze landed on the boy band poster on the wall, tacked up eagerly when she was thirteen and never taken down. Oh, how deeply she'd crushed on every single one of those boys! The cork board above her desk was still packed with the programs and notes and pictures and postcards she'd pinned up her senior year. She smiled at the program from her prom, which she'd gone to with her platonic pal Jimmy, a fellow nerd who now lived in San Francisco. Her gaze wandered to a photo of herself and her best friend Kelly, who was now married and living a few towns away, the proud mom of an adorable eight-month-old boy who had recently discovered his crawling superpowers. Next to the photo was a to-do list — a reminder of where her head was the spring of her senior year. Number one on the list: "Pack for New York."

She sighed, and her attention wandered to the three pieces of artwork that hung in a row above her bed. She'd done the pieces herself, in art class her sophomore year with the encouragement of her art teacher and her dad, who had insisted she hang them up. The first was a watercolor landscape of Heart-springs Lake on a grey winter day, a lone skater gliding over the ice. There was an undeniable sadness hovering over the figure on the lake, a loneli-ness echoed in the gray emptiness of the surround-ings. The second painting, done in oil, was the view from Clara's bedroom window of the oak tree in the front yard, its branches bare of leaves, the sky again a soft gray. Like the skater on the lake, the tree appeared bereft, even hopeless, in the face of the coldness surrounding it.

The third piece was a line drawing, a charcoal sketch done from memory, of her mom, sitting in the rocking chair in her bedroom, gazing at the oak tree in the front yard. Her face was thinned out and a scarf was wrapped around her head, but her expres-sion conveyed both sadness and resolve. Somehow, Clara had managed to capture her mother's truth in that moment — an acceptance of what was coming, but also a determination to continue living all the life she had left to live.

The three pieces, done in the months following her mom's passing, had never been about creating art. They'd been about escape and consolation. They'd been a method, a tool, for Clara to channel her grief by focusing on something concrete, some-thing physical, to anchor her as she pushed her way through her overwhelming loss.

She hadn't realized what the art pieces were about, not at the time. But her art teacher had, and so had her dad.

Her mattress squeaked and she felt herself return to the here and now. She took another deep breath, then sat up. She had so much to do — where to start? She knew from experience that tackling a list of tasks worked best when she started with a simple one. Which meant she should focus on … fixing up the window display. Yes, doing that would be easy enough. It would require her going back to the hardware store, which meant she'd likely encounter Luke, which meant she needed to do something about her face and clothes and….

Gah!

What was she so worried about? She was a grown woman now, not some shy teenager with a hopeless crush. If she got moving now, she'd have time for a quick shower — a reliably hot one this time. Then: Hair and makeup and change of clothes. Then: Call Bert to set up Melody for the concert. Then: Call Abby at the chocolate shop and give her a head's up. Then: Pick up Melody at the Inn and head back to the town square. Then: Tell her dad that, while she appreciated him signing her up for the cookie contest, it just wasn't going to happen. The last thing she needed, in the midst of everything else going on, was worrying about making a batch of contest-winning cookies.

So much to do, and so little time. The story of her life. With a sigh, she stood up and prepared for battle.

CHAPTER 11

Fifty-nine minutes later, Clara gave herself a final once-over in the entry-hall mirror before heading out. For the first time that day, she looked like she actually cared about her appearance. Her curly honey-brown hair was shampooed and straightened. Her complexion was smoothed. Her eyes were lined. Instead of a shapeless sweat-shirt, she had on her favorite sweater, a form-fitting burgundy merino-wool number that she didn't regret splurging on for even one second. The casual blue jeans were gone, replaced by a pair of black slacks that seemed to magically make her legs look longer. Her heavy boots, alas, had to stay — it was winter in Heartsprings Valley, after all, and as a native she knew what that meant.

She picked up a burgundy-and-white holiday scarf and wrapped it around her neck, slipped into her pair of sleek black gloves, and shrugged into her heavy winter coat. With a deep breath, she opened the door and headed out into the crisp afternoon air.

She'd had a productive hour. Bert Winters, the choir director, had been thrilled when she called to tell him about Melody. "We'd love to have her join us," he'd gushed. "Such a huge star, in our midst? Can't wait to meet her." And because Bert was also the town's mayor, he'd turned the conversation to his favorite topic with her: Clara's inevitable future in Heartsprings Valley. "I can't be mayor forever and you've got the drive and can-do spirit for the job," he'd said. "The sooner I can find someone to pass the baton to, the better."

Clara had laughed. "You're always saying that."

"And I mean it. I've finally convinced the town council to hire a town manager. Someone who can work with me and learn the ropes."

She'd laughed again. "Now, now. I'm very happy in New York."

"Well, just think about it, young lady. That's all I'm asking."

Her next call, to Abby at the chocolate shop, had been just as encouraging. "Of course, please have Melody come by!" she'd exclaimed. "I love her. I can't believe it!"

Clara whipped out her newly charged phone again and called Melody. After a ring, her client picked up.

"Hello, darling."

"Melody, I'm on my way there. See you in a few."

"Darling, I'm having such fun with Barbara. She's showing me her recipe for pumpkin pie. Let me put you on speaker."

There was a pause, then Clara heard Barbara say, "Clara, I need to keep Melody here for a while. She's got her video camera out — she says I've got charisma. A star in the making." She laughed heartily.

"Barbara's a natural," Melody said, agreeing immediately. "The queen of her kitchen. Clara, I can't join you right now. We're getting to an important part of the recipe."

They both sounded sincere — like they were enjoying themselves. Clara quickly adjusted the afternoon plan. "Sounds good. I'm on my way to the hardware store to help fix the window display. Melody, how about you join me there when you're ready? I called Abby, who runs the chocolate shop on the square, and she's agreed to a chocolate-making session tomorrow afternoon. I want to take you over there to introduce you."

"We'll be busy here for about another hour," Barbara said.

"Got it," Clara said. "Melody, do you remember how to get to the hardware store?"

"Easy-peasy, darling. See you in a bit. Ta ta!"

"See you soon." As Clara hung up, she heard the

sound of the two women chattering away again happily.

A relieved smile crept to her face. Maybe keeping Melody occupied wasn't going to be as hard as she thought. Maybe her fellow townspeople would help her out. Maybe her client would cooperate as well. She was certainly being very agreeable today — not a single diva-like demand so far. Of course, the day wasn't over. There was still plenty of time for Melody to say, "Clara, darling, I've had the most marvelous little idea…."

As she approached the town square, the side-walks grew more crowded with folks doing last-minute shopping. With just two days till Christmas, there was little time left to get gifts bought and wrapped and placed under the tree. She smiled at the sight of everyone bustling to and fro, loaded with bags full of goodies. All around her, energetic tykes raced up and down the sidewalks, their excitement obvious and adorable. Clara heard one little girl, about six years old, explain to her younger brother, "Santa's coming to town in *two* nights." Her brother replied, "He's coming *tonight*?" The girl said patiently, "No, not tonight. *Tomorrow* night."

Clara grinned. Kids were definitely on her to-do list — someday. But first things first. Employing the crowd-navigating skills she'd perfected in New York, she made her way to the hardware store and paused for a moment outside, her eyes running over the window display, allowing herself to take in the magnitude of the challenge she'd set for herself.

The window display wasn't big — ten feet wide, four feet deep, running from floor to ceiling. But right now, it was definitely a big mess. A ladder had been planted in the center of the space to allow access to the attic crawlspace, presumably to deal with the heating problem.

Surely there was a different spot for the ladder to gain entry to the attic? The window display was important. With a quick look at her reflection in the window, she took a deep breath and headed in.

Peggy, who was ringing up a customer at a cash register, saw her and smiled. "Welcome back, Clara."

"Thanks, Peggy. If it's all right with you, I'll get started on the window display."

"Perfect. Want to leave your coat behind the counter?"

Clara shrugged out of her coat, stepped behind the counter, and stuffed it in a cubby under the cash register. As she did so, she realized again: Without the heater going strong, the store felt downright *chilly*. She almost changed her mind about taking off her coat before she remembered how good her sweater looked.

"I think I'll keep the gloves on."

"Good call," Peggy said. "Holler if you need anything."

"Will do."

Clara made her way to the back of the window display, then pulled open the display's small door and stepped in. Looking up, she saw that the ladder was placed below one of the access hatches for the crawlspace. The hatch was open. She gripped the ladder in both hands and made her way up.

As she neared the top, she was able to peek into the crawlspace. Her nose scrunched in distaste. She'd been up here a few times as a kid, but crawlspaces had never been her thing — way too dark and spider-filled for her liking.

Stale, musty air assailed her nostrils. Across the space, about twenty feet away, someone lay on his side next to what looked like the heating system, aiming a flashlight at it, his boots pointed her way.

She cleared her throat. "Luke, is that you?"

"Yep," he said, then shifted position so that he could see her. "Clara, that you?"

"You need anything from me?"

"Not right now. Just working out a plan of attack."

So he likes plans, too —just like me. She swatted away the thought.

"When you have a minute, can we talk about the window display?" she said.

"Sure. There in a minute."

She made her way down the ladder and waited. Above her, she heard bumps and scrapes as he crawled toward her. Boots appeared in the hatch above her, followed by blue jeans and a red plaid flannel shirt.

And then, suddenly, he was next to her, a bit closer than would be normal due to the confines of the tiny space. She'd forgotten how tall he was — a bit north of six feet — and how solid. She had to stretch her neck to stare into those shockingly blue eyes.

"I didn't recognize you at first," he said, gazing upon her, his eyes alive with curiosity.

"Is that so?"

"The last time I saw you was back in high school. Ten years ago."

Fluttering nervousness returned full-force. "Is that so?" she said again, cursing herself for being so tongue-tied.

"You're all grown up now," he said with a grin.

Yes, she was. And the problem was, so was he. And the problem was, he was standing really close to her right now in this small space, close enough for her to be very aware of not only his flannel shirt but also a hint of his aftershave.

And he was being so nice and attentive. *Gah!*

Even when he'd been the star quarterback and the cutest and most popular boy in school, he'd never acted like a stereotypical high-school jock. There'd never been any arrogance in him, never any expectation that he should be treated differently or better than anyone else. His parents had raised him well.

No, the problem was that he was so darned *handsome*. If only that short-cropped blond hair of his wasn't practically begging for her to run her fingers through it. If only his voice wasn't so deep with a hint of roughness. He'd shaved that morning, but already she saw a hint of stubble on that strong jaw of his.

Gah! She needed distance if she was going to get her brain back in working order.

"So…" she said, trying to keep any hint of desperation out of her voice. "Why don't we step out of here for a second?"

"Sure," he said agreeably. "After you."

She twisted around and slipped out of the tight space, Luke following. She found a spot in an aisle next to a display of sparkling Christmas tree decorations and took a breath to calm herself down. "You mentioned a plan of attack. What's it looking like up there?"

"Well," he said, his face becoming more serious, "it's an old system, probably older than we are. Some point soon, your dad will want to replace it with something more energy-efficient. You'll see savings on your monthly heating bill immediately."

"That makes sense," she replied, relieved to be talking about something specific and non-personal. "But for now?"

"For now, we stick with what we've got."

"And the diagnosis?"

"We need to replace one of the parts — the thermocouple pilot light."

"Which means?"

"First question is, what kinds of thermocouples do you have here?"

"We can check. If we don't have the kind we need?"

"Then I'll make some calls."

Okay, this was encouraging. She was having a rational, reasonable conversation with her high-school crush without breaking into a sweat or clamming up or fleeing. She was holding his gaze and, apparently, his interest. Amazing what a decade of growing up could do.

"So," she said, "can I switch the topic?"

"Sure."

"We need to do something about the window display."

"Ah," he said, understanding immediately.

"Can we move the ladder out of there?"

He sighed. "Here's the problem. The window display is one of only three entry points for the crawlspace. Let me show you the others."

He led her to the Customer Assistance station at the other end of the aisle, where several customers were getting help from employees. He pointed to an access hatch above the help desk. "If we put up the ladder here, we'll get in the way of the help desk and customers."

"Agreed, we can't do that," she said as she peered up. "Isn't there an access point in the storeroom?"

He nodded. "Let me show you."

They made their way through the store toward the back room, navigating customers at nearly every step.

"You guys do a great business here," he said to her over his shoulder.

"Christmas is crazy," she agreed.

Finally, they got to the storeroom. Boxes filled with all manner of goods lined both sides of the entry passage, positioned to be easily available when items needed to be restocked on shelves up front.

"Usually, there isn't as much stuff in here," she said as she took in the stacks of boxes.

"That's Christmas for you."

At that moment, her dad walked in. "Hi, honey," he said, giving her a quick kiss on the cheek. "You get Melody settled in?"

"She's with Barbara, making pumpkin pie. Right now, I'm trying to figure out the window display."

"Good."

"Which means figuring out the ladder."

Her dad turned to Luke. "When I was up there this morning, it looked like the problem was the thermocouple."

Luke nodded. "Yep, that's it."

"I just checked, and we don't have the right one

here. I can order it, but it won't get here until after Christmas."

"Let me make a call or two — I might be able to get it sooner."

"That'd be great."

"Dad," Clara said, "about the window display."

Her dad eased between them, opened a box stacked next to them, and pulled out two cans of paint. "Whatever you two come up with is fine. But make sure the ladder isn't in the way back here, especially right here. Too much movement in and out." He gave her a smile. "Gotta get this paint out there." He turned and left.

Wordlessly, Luke pointed up, and her eyes followed. Directly above them was the third access hatch for the crawlspace.

He shrugged. "Sorry."

Urgh.

As the magnitude of the problem settled in, she felt her organizing instincts kick into high gear. Clearly, Luke had considered the three available options for ladder placement, and had selected the spot that was least disruptive to customers and employees. She respected that — it showed he was a problem-solver, like her. But had he given proper weight to the importance of the window display, especially with Christmas just two days away? Not if he was anything like her dad, who always delegated the window display to his employees and never said anything more than "Looks terrific!" when he saw the result.

She sighed. "The problem is that the window display is super-important."

He nodded. "I'm open to suggestions." He stood there, his attention fully focused on her, waiting for her to respond.

She became aware that it was just the two of them in the storeroom. Suddenly the space felt claustrophobic. "Let's go back out there," she said, gesturing toward the front.

"Sure." He turned and headed out, and she followed.

They found a spot in the plumbing aisle, which, like every other aisle in the store, was packed with customers. A random thought came as she watched two people in a row pick up a faucet shank extender: *Why were people buying faucet shank extenders with Christmas just around the corner? Perhaps they had holiday guests and wanted everything ship-shape before their guests arrived? Perhaps they were buying faucet shank extenders because their loved ones really liked them? Perhaps they remembered they needed faucet shank extenders only after coming to the store to buy holiday lights or candy canes or a new mixer or a wreath for the front door?*

Perhaps, she realized, she was fixating on faucet shank extenders because she was *stalling*? For time and for inspiration? Because she had no idea how to solve the supposedly simple problem — the window display — she'd tasked herself with?

"I suppose we can't move the ladder away and bring it back only as needed?" she asked, even though she already knew the answer.

"Sorry," he said with a grin. "If I could fly, maybe. But flying isn't one of my superpowers."

"You have superpowers?" she replied, arching an eyebrow.

He grinned. "Only a couple. Like: I'm pretty good at fixing stuff."

"You're also pretty good at wrecking window displays."

His grin grew wider. "Only in service to the greater good." He leaned closer. "I bet I can guess your superpower."

"Oh, is that so?"

"Your superpower is … the ability to find the possible in impossible situations."

She liked the sound of that. She liked the sound of that *a lot*. In fact, she realized, she was liking everything about this encounter. Without warning, she became fifteen again, gawky and awkward and shy. She felt her cheeks flame red.

"Listen," he said, shifting gears, either oblivious to her inner turmoil or considerately offering her a way through it. "I want to help. I get it — that display window needs to be the best it can be for Christmas."

She felt herself calming again as the danger zone

of semi-flirting receded in the rear-view mirror. "Yes, it's important," she said. "But we also need the heater up and running so our customers aren't shivering when they're standing in line at the cash register."

"Right."

"Which means the ladder isn't going away until the heater is fixed."

"Right."

She blinked. "So what's the ETA on the fix?"

He pulled his phone out of his pocket. "Let me make a call or two and find out."

CHAPTER 12

Clara returned to the window display while Luke made his calls. She stepped back into the tiny space, her eyes roving, her mind wandering. The "A" ladder was so big, and it was placed dead-center — truly, an inescapable and immovable reality. She felt the glimmerings of an idea forming when the door squeaked open. She turned and saw Peggy peering in.

"Hey," Peggy said. "Checking in. Any ideas?"

"Not yet, but I'm getting there."

"Thank you again for your help with this. What's Luke say about the heater?"

"He needs a certain part. Dad checked and we don't have it here, so Luke's making calls."

Peggy shivered. "Getting the heat back will be such a relief."

"I completely agree."

"Thank goodness he's able to help. The two of you knew each other back in high school, right?"

"Yes and no," Clara said. "I knew who he was — star quarterback and all. But I was three years behind him, so he didn't really know me."

Luke appeared. "Good news. Jim's got the part we need. I can drive over now and get it."

"I'm so glad to hear that," Peggy said. "Clara, why don't you go with him? You kids can get reacquainted."

Luke blinked, startled.

Clara said, "Oh, I don't think —"

"Now, now," Peggy said to them with a reassuring smile. "You two have a lot to talk about. You've both done such interesting things since high school."

Clara opened her mouth, then closed it. *Go on a ride? With the most popular boy in Heartsprings Valley High?* She couldn't —

"Sure," Luke said, then turned to her with a question in his eyes. "I'm game if you are."

Gah! Was this really happening? The answer popped out of her mouth before she could stop herself. "Okay. Sure. Yes, that would be fine."

He grinned and checked his pockets and pulled out his keys. "I'm ready. You?"

More calmly than she thought possible, she said, "Let me get my coat."

She squeezed past him and Peggy and walked to the counter. Peggy followed and, as Clara reached down to get her coat, said, "I hope it's okay that I suggested you two spend a bit of time together."

Clara stood up and faced the other woman. Although she didn't know Peggy well, she recognized a fellow planner — a fellow creator of opportunities. After all, the fine art of meddling was a specialty in Heartsprings Valley. As a native, she knew all of the ins and outs, having absorbed the techniques effortlessly while growing up. She opened her mouth to respond, then shut it when she realized she didn't know how she felt about Peggy's suggestion. Or, more bluntly, about her meddling. Except that wasn't true. If she was being honest with herself, she was …

Pleased by it.

Yes, pleased. Also flustered and nervous. The jolt of anticipation had been undeniable.

She took a deep breath, then surprised herself again by saying, "How long have you and my dad been dating?"

Now it was Peggy's turn to blink and take a deep breath. "Three months," she said after a short pause. A look of anxiety appeared on her face, her warm brown eyes searching Clara's face for an indication of how Clara felt.

"Are you two serious?"

Peggy nodded. "Yes, it is. I mean, we are. He's a wonderful man. I take it your dad told you?"

"No, not yet. My guess is, he's planning to tell me

tonight, at home."

Peggy gave her a tentative smile. "Was it … obvious that we're dating?"

"Just little hints here and there. It took me a little while to sort them out."

Peggy nodded. "I want you to know that your dad and I are taking things slowly. Neither of us is rushing into anything. We're taking the time to get to know each other. It's been a while for both us. We're a bit" — she struggled for the right word — "rusty."

The word brought a smile to Clara's lips. There was something touching about Peggy's admission. Something human and real. She realized she liked this woman. Even if she wasn't sure how she felt about her dad going on dates. Of course she wanted her dad to be happy. But still, he was her dad….

"I forgive you," Clara said.

"Forgive me?" Peggy replied, brow furrowing.

"For suggesting I go with Luke to get the part."

"Ah," Peggy said, breaking into a relieved smile. "Good."

"And," Clara said, reaching out to take Peggy's hands in hers. "I want you to know — I'm glad my dad's dating. I know we don't know each other very well yet, but I'm looking forward to getting to know you."

"I'm so glad to hear that, Clara," Peggy said, gratitude and relief in her voice. "I look forward to getting to know you, too."

CHAPTER 13

*W*ith a smile, Clara shrugged into her heavy winter coat, zipped herself in, and wrapped her scarf around her neck. "Back soon." She headed to the store entrance, where Luke was waiting.

He grinned as she approached. "My truck's parked across the street."

Together they made their way to a big beefy black pickup with "Matthews Contracting" stenciled on the side, along with a phone number and email address.

Luke looked ready to scoot around to open the passenger door for her, but Clara shooed him off and opened the door herself. "Is the company just you and your dad?" she asked as she climbed in.

"Depends on the job," Luke said as he hopped behind the wheel. They closed their doors and buckled up. "We bring in subcontractors as needed."

He slid the key into the ignition and the truck roared to life, the engine letting out a hearty rumble. "For the day-to-day, yeah, it's me or Dad managing a job."

"You don't have a heating expert?"

"We do, but Ed's been working overtime on a job at the high school and he's looking forward to a few days off with his family for Christmas, so I took on the hardware store job instead."

"That's very considerate of you."

He glanced at her, then carefully pulled out. "We're a team. We all pitch in where we can."

He'd said it in such a matter-of-fact way. Like it was a truth ingrained in him.

"How far away is this Jim guy with the part?"

"About fifteen minutes."

He turned off the town square and headed down the road that led out of town into the heart of the valley. Most of the homes they passed were decorated for the season with strings of lights and snowmen and more.

Luke handled the truck easily and with confidence, his touch on the wheel light but assured, his attention never straying more than a second from the road. She glanced around the cabin. Everything was neat and well-ordered. No fast-food wrappers on the floor, no half-drunk coffee cups in the holder, no stains, no doodads hanging from the rear-view mirror. That made sense, given what she'd noticed about him already — his preference for planning, his attention to detail, his get-the-job-done attitude....

"Your truck is really clean," she said, then immediately regretted it. *Why had she said that?*

"Thanks. I don't like messes. Messes bug me."

"Me, too."

He smiled. "You know what Aunt Peggy's up to, right?"

She grinned, relieved he'd said it. "You mean, suggesting we spend time together?"

He chuckled. "Don't get me wrong — I'm happy to spend time with you. But I don't want you to feel awkward because of that."

"Thanks," she replied. "Totally agree." Though at the same time, the thought came: *How am I going to avoid feeling awkward around you when my brain refuses to think clearly in your presence?*

"We're heading to the salvage yard," he said.

"I remember that place," she said, relieved he'd found a safe topic of conversation. "Back when I was a kid, my friends and I used to play hide-and-seek there."

"Me and my friends did the same. Kind of a rite of passage for us Heartsprings Valley kids."

She hadn't thought about the old salvage yard in years. Memories came flooding back of hot summer days, playing amidst the stacks of old cars, farm machinery, and logging equipment. She remembered dandelions springing up next to rusting hulks, the scents of oil and dust mixing with the aroma of fertilizer from nearby farms, grasshoppers jumping to and fro. Everything back then had seemed so fascinating and strange to her young eyes.

"Is there an old heating system out there we're going to plunder?" she asked.

"Yep. A few days ago, we brought the old heater from the high school out there. Luckily for us, Jim hasn't sold or scrapped it yet. I'm pretty sure we can take the thermocouple from that system and use it at the hardware store."

"Perfect."

They passed the same snow hippo that Clara had noticed on the bus ride into town, and saw Luke grinning.

"That hippo cracks me up," he said. "Every time I see it."

"Me, too. I saw it this morning."

"On the bus from New York, right?"

"Yep."

"Tell me more about what you do there. You said PR, right?"

"I work for a small agency. Very small — just my boss Nigel and me."

"Your boss — what's he like?"

"Very smart, very experienced, very English."

"An Englishman?"

"He's lived in New York for more than twenty

years — he moved there when he met his wife, who's American. They have three kids now, all teenagers."

"Is he a good guy?"

"Very much so. He works hard, he's committed to his clients, and he's always coming up with new ideas and plans. I've learned so much working for him."

"So … he's the mentor and you're the apprentice."

"Exactly."

"How long now?"

"Two years."

"Do you focus on certain areas?"

She nodded. "Mostly clients in the entertainment industry who want or need to change their media coverage."

"People like Melody Connelly."

"Right. She's up here to do a series of video blog posts."

"Let me guess: She wants to show her fans that she's more than just a big-time Broadway star. She wants to come across as … relatable?"

"Exactly," Clara said, impressed.

"She'll be fine. She seems nice enough." He glanced toward her. "Is she?"

"Oh, she is. She's quite nice in person, and generous with charitable causes — always willing to make appearances or perform to raise money. Nigel and I have worked with a couple of big stars — who shall remain nameless, thank you very much — who

are most definitely *not* nice. But Melody's mostly
very good to work with."

"Mostly?" Luke replied, shooting her a quick
glance.

"I should rephrase. I don't want to give the wrong
impression. She's great. It's just that sometimes she
asks for stuff that's super-tough to pull together."

"Stuff like what?" He seemed genuinely
interested.

She took a deep breath. "Well, the example that
springs to mind is the elephant."

"The elephant?" he said, startled.

She told him the tale of the red-carpet elephant.
He laughed and shook his head, clearly enjoying her
story.

"Impossible demands," he said. "I can relate."

She smiled. "You were in the Army, right?"

"Eight years."

"What did you do?"

"I fixed stuff and built stuff." He began to say
more, then found his attention diverted. He
gestured toward a spot ahead on the road. "Here we
are."

She turned and saw the salvage yard on the right.
It covered several acres of land and, as always
seemed to be the case, was filled with old cars and
machinery and equipment of all kinds, now lightly
dusted with snow.

He pulled into a parking space in front of a small

cottage — a shack, really — that served as the salvage yard's office.

"You want to stay in the truck or come with?" he asked as he pulled to a stop.

"I'll come in," she said, curious.

They hopped out. Luke pulled open the door of the shack and a bell tinkled. He ushered her into the front room, which was set up as the office, with a desk and three chairs and a bulletin board on one wall above a string of Christmas lights. A thin, middle-aged man sat behind the desk, his eyes glued to a small TV against the wall, tuned into a cooking show.

"Hey, Jim," Luke said.

"You seen how they do this?" Jim said, unable to tear his attention away from the TV screen, where the cook was making a pie. "I've always wondered how to make a pecan pie."

The room, though looking decidedly worn, was at least toasty warm. Clara felt herself relaxing as the heat seeped in. They watched Jim and the TV screen as the cooking show host carefully poured the golden pecan mixture into the pie. A minute later, when the show went to a commercial, Jim turned toward them.

"Sorry," he said. "I'm surprising the wife with a new dessert for Christmas dinner. Now I know how to make it." His face, thin and angular, broke into a pleased grin. He was dressed in coveralls, with a blue wool sweater underneath. Gradually, he realized that

Luke wasn't his only visitor. His eyes took in Clara with interest, then with puzzlement.

"I know you," he said to her. "You're Ted's daughter. Moved to New York."

"That's right. Clara Cane."

His brow cleared, and his glance moved to Luke. "That part you need — it's for the hardware store?"

Luke nodded. "They have the same system we pulled out of the high school last week."

Jim slowly stood up and straightened out his back with a small groan. "Sitting too long. Let's head to the barn." They followed him through the cottage — which, aside from the front room, consisted of a small kitchen, bathroom, and storage room — and out the back door and toward a big red barn.

He turned to Clara. "We do most of our sorting and cataloguing back here." He pulled open the barn door and let them in. Clara's eyes widened. Stalls that had once been home to cows and horses were now lined with shelves of carefully reclaimed items. She stepped closer to a shelf filled with rows of small metal buckets. In each bucket were nails of a certain size. Other shelves had buckets full of bolts, nuts, tacks, screws and more, all meticulously sorted.

"This stuff used to get tossed into garbage dumps," Jim said, stepping closer. "A terrible waste."

"I imagine you do a good business," she said as her gaze took in the rows of stalls.

"A nice profit — well worth the effort of sorting it.

There's a lot of life left in these old parts. Makes me feel good, knowing they're being put to their intended use again."

Luke walked to the back of the barn, to an area that appeared to be reserved for new arrivals. "This where the heater is?"

Jim nodded. "Haven't been able to tackle it yet. Lucky for you. Getting parts for older systems isn't easy."

"You're not kidding." Luke's eyes landed on something and lit up. "Here we go." He picked up what looked like a metal box and said, "What we need should be in here."

"Great," Jim said and gestured toward a nearby table.

She watched the two men focus on the box. Luke took a screwdriver from Jim and quickly had the box open. He applied the screwdriver to another screw inside the box, then carefully pulled out what looked like a jumble of wires leading into a tiny wand. "This is what we're after," he said.

"This is a … thermocouple?" Clara asked, her curiosity piqued.

"Yep."

"Don't new systems have the same kind of thing?"

"They do, but not the same size. Your dad's system uses one with these dimensions. We could have come up with a temporary solution using a different one, but this is a better fit." He examined it carefully. "And it's in good shape. It should hold up until your dad replaces the system."

"Which will be when?"

"I'm thinking sometime in the spring. We'll have to take the heater out of commission for a couple of days while we get the old system out and the new system in, so we'll wait until the temperatures are milder." He gave her a grin. "Don't want your customers shivering again."

"Amen to that."

He turned to Jim. "What do I owe you?"

"Nothing," Jim said with a wave of his hand. "Consider it a Christmas gift."

"You sure?"

"More than sure, given all the business you bring me." Jim turned to Clara. "Welcome back, young lady. I hope we'll be seeing more of you."

"I'm here just for a short visit," she replied, though she realized, as the words came out of her mouth, that saying them made her feel *anxious*. Like she felt when she said something that wasn't true. Which was odd, because the words were true. Most definitely. She was definitely here for just a short visit.

"Sorry to hear that," Jim said. "Guess I figured wrong."

She blinked, startled, and saw Luke shoot him a puzzled look.

"Figured what wrong?" she asked.

"That you two were an item. You know —
dating."

Her eyes widened with surprise.

"You look right for each other, is all," he continued, looking right at her. "Plus I thought, if you
weren't dating him, why would you be going with
him to a salvage yard on the outskirts of town to get
a part for a heating system on a cold winter day two
days before Christmas?"

Clara's mouth opened, but no words came out.
When Jim put it that way, it was kind of hard to
argue the point.

"We ... I ... we haven't seen each other in a
decade," she said, feeling her face turn red.

"We're just getting reacquainted," Luke added
quickly. "We met again today, when I went to the
hardware store to help with their heating system."

"Whatever you say," Jim said, clearly
unconvinced.

Luke shook his head. "You're just as bad as
everyone else."

"Bad?" Jim said innocently.

"Everyone in this town is a natural-born meddler.
It's like there's something in the water."

Clara grinned, glad that Luke was so willing to
say out loud what she herself had been thinking.

Jim seemed unperturbed by Luke's assertion. He
turned to Clara. "Luke's been on our minds for a

while now. We've introduced him to several young ladies."

Luke said, "Jim —"

"But you're the first young lady he's brought out here," Jim said with a grin. "You're the first young lady he's brought anywhere since he got back, far as I know."

Luke sighed and shook his head, clearly annoyed at how the conversation had turned.

"Jim," Clara said, stepping in, "thank you so much for helping us with the part. We really appreciate it. We have a busy day ahead of us, so we should probably be getting back."

"Nice seeing you again, Clara," Jim said with a warm grin. "Welcome back to Heartsprings Valley."

CHAPTER 14

They were silent at first on the ride back to town, both of them stewing over what Jim had said.

Finally, Clara broke the silence. "I'm glad you spoke up. Really, what we do is no one's business but our own."

"I completely, totally agree," Luke said.

"The way everyone is so determined to get people together is … so annoying."

"Absolutely."

"You and I are grownups. We're not kids anymore. We've seen a lot of the world. We can make our own decisions."

"Exactly."

A feeling of righteousness rose within her. "You and I are capable of making adult choices without my dad or your aunt or the local salvage-yard operator trying to manipulate us."

"Amen," Luke said, banging on the steering wheel for emphasis. "Here's to freedom!"

"Yes, freedom!"

They looked at each other for a long second, then burst into laughter.

"For the record," he said after he caught his breath, "even though I'm very firmly anti-meddling, I'm glad we're getting to hang out. You're fun, Clara Cane."

"Thank you," she said, aware of the flush of pleasure at his words. "I'm glad, too. I'm happy to hang out with you."

"Good," he said, his blue eyes alive with warmth.

She surprised herself by keeping her eyes on his. "Even though you totally destroyed the window display."

"Hey," he said, mock-protesting. "A sacrifice for the greater good."

"Speaking of the window display, I've got an idea for how to make it all work — a way for you to have access to the crawlspace and me to get the window decorated — but it will involve keeping your ladder in place until the display gets updated after the New Year."

"A plan. You've got a plan."

"I think so, yes."

"Which requires holding my ladder hostage?"

"Yes. If that's okay."

"No problem. Though it sounds like I don't have much choice."

She grinned. "None at all. Glad we're on the same page."

He chuckled, and their talk switched to the inevitable "whatever-happened-to" conversations of every high school reunion. Clara felt herself relaxing, the back-and-forth flowing easily, her uncomfortable awareness of his attractiveness beginning to recede as she saw more of what was inside — his curiosity, his sense of humor, his courtesy toward her. Before she knew it, he was pulling into a parking spot across the street from the hardware store and turning off the engine.

"We're back," he said.

"You know," she said, not ready to leave the truck, "we still haven't talked about you — what you did in the Army."

"Happy to tell you all about it."

"You said you fixed stuff?"

He nodded. "All kinds of stuff. You name it, I probably fixed it, upgraded it, built it, or tore it down." He gestured toward the store. "Including a heating system or two. Hey, look who's here."

Her eyes followed his. To her dismay, she saw Melody walking up the sidewalk toward the hardware store. Apparently, her client's baking adventure with Barbara had ended.

He noticed her frown. "We should get in there."

"Yes," she said with a sigh.

"I've got a heater to fix."

"And I've got a client to manage and a window display to put together."

CHAPTER 15

*R*eluctantly, Clara unbuckled, pushed open the door, and hopped out of the truck. Together, she and Luke made their way across the street. The hardware store was as busy as it had been earlier, with customers crowding every aisle and a long line to check out. Peggy, now bundled in a thick white wool sweater, was ringing up a customer at one of the registers.

"I'm gonna find your dad," Luke said.

"Sounds good." She watched him head to the back of the store, then waited for Peggy to finish with her customer before squeezing behind the counter. "Hey, Peggy, we're back."

Peggy looked over her shoulder as Clara scooted past and gave her a welcoming smile. "Success?"

"I think so." Clara unzipped her coat, then shrugged it off and stuffed it under the counter. "We went to the salvage yard. Luke got a part from the high school's old heating system that he thinks will do the trick."

"Good," Peggy said with a shiver. "We need the heat! I'm turning into a popsicle."

"I saw Melody walk in. You know where she is?"

"I didn't notice her, sorry."

"No worries. I'll find her. I have an idea for the window display, and I'm going to see if Melody wants to help out."

"Thank you so much for pitching in, Clara."

"Happy to — I'm enjoying it."

Which was a true statement, she realized. Even though part of her still longed for a restful, lazy, sleep-filled Christmas, today's whirlwind of activity had been rather fun.

She slid past Peggy, then made her way down the crowded plumbing aisle toward a sound she recognized all too well: her client's throaty laugh. She found Melody with her dad and Luke at the end of the aisle, the three of them still laughing at something one of them had said.

"Darling," Melody said, her lovely green eyes flashing when she spied Clara. "I've just been telling your father and Luke about my pumpkin-pie adventure with Barbara."

"It went well?"

"You have no idea! Barbara's a natural in front of the camera. And such a wonderful baker."

"And you got some footage for your blog?"

Melody gave Clara's shoulders a squeeze. "Wonderful footage. Full of life and laughter. Darling, I'm so glad to be here in this delightful town."

When Melody was in a good mood — bubbly and effervescent, brimming with brio — Clara had learned to ride the wave. "If you're game, I have something else for us to do. Not as tasty as pie in Barbara's kitchen, but just as Christmas-y."

"Spill, dear."

"Have you ever done a Christmas display for a store window?"

Melody's eyes lit up. "You mean…?"

"Yes. Right here. Right now."

Her client whipped out her phone. "Ready to roll, darling."

Clara turned to her dad and Luke. "Is the ladder placed where you need it?"

Luke gave her a grin. "I think I know what you're planning."

"Oh, you do?"

"Yep. And I like it. Just leave me a way to step up and down, and whatever you've got planned will be fine."

"I might need you to step up and down carefully."

"No problem."

Her dad said, "Well, you two seem to know what you're talking about. Even if I don't."

"It'll be good, Dad, don't worry." Clara turned to

Melody. "Time to get to work." She led her client to the aisle overflowing with Christmas supplies and decorations. "First, we need our materials."

"What kind of materials?"

"Christmas lights. A string of colored lights. And garlands of tinsel."

"What color tinsel?"

"Green. Definitely green."

"A traditional Christmas look," Melody murmured. "Not sleek or all-white or silver or modern."

"Yes, that's right. Something warm, something that hearkens back."

Melody plucked a big bag of dark-green tinsel from a high shelf. "Like this?"

"Perfect," Clara said, then reached down and pulled up a package of colorful Christmas lights. "The tinsel will look great with these lights." She paused. "We need one more thing. Let's go to the housewares aisle."

Together, they made their way to the aisle stuffed with curtains and pillows and blankets and area rugs and bathroom mats and more.

"What are we after?" Melody asked.

"Shower curtains, blankets, or sheets. Some type of red or green."

"Ah…."

Clara ran her eyes over the selection. They would need several large pieces of fabric, she realized. The display window was ten feet long and probably nine feet high — bigger than any single piece of fabric.

She noticed Melody eyeing a shower curtain that depicted a wintry outdoor landscape of pine trees gently dusted with snow. Her client gave her an inquiring look. "Can we use this?"

Indeed they could. Clara's heart started beating faster when she spied window curtains of deep burgundy red. She stepped closer and ran her hand over the rich red fabric.

"What do you think?" she asked Melody.

Melody nodded. "Darling, that will be perfect."

They grabbed the shower curtain and window curtains and carried their materials to the window display.

"We'll need something to hang them up with," Melody said.

"Back in a sec," Clara replied. She zipped down the tool aisle, picked up a hammer, then made her way to a wall dedicated to nails and screws and hooks of all sorts and selected what she needed.

She brought her bundle back to Melody. "I'll get started."

She stepped inside the display space, climbed up the ladder, and popped her head inside the crawl-space. Through the musty gloom, she saw Luke lying on his side next to the heater, already at work. "Is it okay if I use the ladder for a few minutes? I'll put it back when I'm done."

"Sure, no problem," he said. "I'll holler if I need it."

"Got it."

She stepped down and carefully repositioned the ladder next to the left side of the wall. With a hammer in one hand and a nail in the other, she climbed up, positioned the nail at the top of the back wall of the display area, slid a nail through the hook, and placed the hook on the wall. She gave it a careful look — yes, she'd placed it in the right spot — and started hammering. With just three efficient swings, the nail and hook were firmly attached.

She let out a satisfied sigh. As the daughter of a hardware store owner, she'd learned from an early age to be comfortable with tools of all sorts. Some skills, like wielding a hammer, were like riding a bike — never forgotten.

Melody, who had watched Clara silently, had the next hook and nail ready. She handed them to her with a smile. "You swing that like a pro. What can you *not* do, Clara Cane?"

"Oh, gosh, lots. Believe me." The next few minutes flew by as Clara nailed and Melody provided, the two of them moving the ladder as needed.

When the final hook was in, Clara stepped back and surveyed her work. "Let's get the shower curtain up." With Melody's help, she got the snowy scene hanging over the center part of the back wall.

Melody handed the first of the two thick red curtains to Clara, who began hanging it to the left of the shower curtain. They followed that by hanging the second red curtain to the right of the shower curtain.

"I'll run out front and see how it looks," Melody said. A few seconds later, she was on the sidewalk, grinning and giving Clara a thumb's up.

Clara climbed down from the ladder and put it back under the access hatch in the center of the display space. Melody popped back in. "It's looking good," she said. "But I think we need to pull the curtains back a bit."

"I'll look for something to tie them," Clara said. "In the meantime, why don't you get started on the tinsel?"

"Wrapped to cover everything?" Melody asked.

Clara nodded, pleased that Melody knew without asking what Clara wanted. Of course, given her client's theater experience, it made sense that Melody understood what Clara planned to do with the tinsel and lights.

It was, however, a bit surprising that Melody was so willing to follow Clara's lead. Her client was typically more take-charge. Usually, she'd be offering Clara lots of "marvelous little ideas." But so far that day, even with a prime opportunity for diva-like behavior with the window display, she'd been as silent and compliant as a mouse. Why was that?

"Melody," Clara said, reaching out and touching her shoulder, "thank you so much for helping out."

"Oh," Melody replied, her face flushing pink. "No need to thank me."

"Well, I *want* to thank you. It's very nice of you, pitching in like this."

Melody smiled. "One doesn't pass up the opportunity to do a Christmas window display, darling. Everyone in New York will be green with envy."

"You should get some of this on video."

"Oh, good call." Melody pulled her phone out of her pocket, licked her lips, brushed back her hair, and aimed the camera at herself. "Right now, I'm squeezed inside the window display at Cane Hardware, a thriving store in the town square right here in Heartsprings Valley." She swung the camera toward Clara. "This charming young woman is Clara Cane, daughter of store owner Ted Cane. Say hello to everyone, Clara."

"Hello, everyone," Clara said, instantly regretting reminding Melody to get video footage.

Melody swung the camera back toward herself. "Sadly, the Christmas window display at Cane Hardware had to be torn asunder when the store's heating system went kaput just two days before Christmas. But Clara has a plan to bring the display back to life, and I'm here to help make that happen."

She turned off the camera. "How does that sound?"

"It sounds perfect," Clara said. And it did. Melody was a professional — she knew exactly what she needed to deliver, and did so effortlessly. "I assume you'll get a bunch of shots of us doing various things…."

"That's right, darling," Melody said as she ran her camera over the display's current unfinished state. "And add voiceover later."

"Is that how it went at the Inn with Barbara?"

"The second I turned the camera on her, she lit up. I couldn't get her to stop mugging for the camera. She had me in stitches."

Clara laughed. "She's always been upbeat, but I didn't know she had such an affinity for the spotlight."

"She didn't either."

"I was about to go get something…. What was it?"

"Ties," Melody said. "For the curtains."

"Right." She stepped past Melody and returned to the housewares section, looking for a red sash or two. But no — nothing there. Then an idea came for what she could use instead. She dashed to the Christmas accessories aisle and grabbed a long length of dark red ribbon.

She took the ribbon back to the display window and showed it to Melody. "This will work, right?"

"Perfect," Melody said.

"We'll need two more hooks on the side walls. Where did I put that hammer?"

"On the floor over there. I'll get you a nail and hook."

They made short work of the task. Melody picked up a piece of red ribbon and used it to pull the left curtain toward the wall. "Too much? Not enough?"

"Let me go outside and check." Clara slipped past Melody and out the store and onto the sidewalk. The late-afternoon sun was dipping toward the horizon; she shivered as a gust of wintry wind penetrated her sweater. Clasping her arms together to protect herself from the frigid air, she looked at the display and how the red curtain was tied halfway down, pulling it back to reveal the snowy scene on the shower curtain. Melody was looking at her through the window, waiting for a signal. Clara gave her a thumb's up and scooted back inside.

"Gosh, it's cold out there," Clara said when she got back to the window display.

"You aren't kidding," Melody said.

Together, they added a tie for the remaining curtain, making a few adjustments to get it just right.

"Does that do it for our backdrop?" Melody asked.

"I think so," Clara replied. "And you know what that means."

Melody grinned. "Time to decorate a tree!"

CHAPTER 16

*A*h, tree decoration. Truly one of her favorite Christmas traditions. For a second, Clara flashed to her little studio apartment in Brooklyn, silent and dark and devoid of yuletide cheer. How sad that she'd been too busy for even a quick trip to the corner deli to pick out a string of lights to drape over her desk / dining table. Even a single decoration would have brought the spirit of the season to her tiny place. But no, she'd been too wrapped up in her job and its never-ending demands on her energy and attention.

At least here in Heartsprings Valley she had time for Christmas. And time for an activity — tree decorating — that never failed to brighten her spirits. Of course, she'd never dealt with a tree quite like the one she was about to tackle.

Melody eyed the aluminum ladder that would

soon be transformed. "Is it positioned right?" she asked.

"I think so," Clara replied. "Let me go up and make sure Luke doesn't need it."

She climbed up and poked her head into the crawlspace. "Luke, we're about to start on the tree. You okay?"

"I'm good," he said from his spot next to the heater, where he was tapping on something gently with a wrench.

"How's it going?"

"Slower than expected. Don't worry, I'll work it out."

"Holler if you need help."

"Will do."

She made her way down and turned to Melody. "We're on."

Together, they opened the bags of green tinsel garland.

"I love this," Melody said. "Look how it sparkles when it catches the light."

Clara nodded. "I think we have enough to wrap the whole thing."

"Easily," Melody said with a grin.

Tinsel in hand, they started wrapping the ladder. Gradually, the aluminum frame disappeared beneath a sparkly green covering and a different object began to emerge, triangular in shape, rising from a wide base to a pointy top.

"This is going to be so great," Melody said, her eyes alive with pleasure.

As Clara watched her client apply herself to the wrapping work, she realized that Melody the star had become, at least for a moment, a different version of herself, perhaps closer to the person she'd been before fame engulfed her. Right now, she was simply a woman immersing herself in holiday pleasures and pitching in on a shared effort.

Again, the thought came: Why was her client here, two days before Christmas?

She'll tell me if she wants to, Clara told herself as she climbed the ladder to wrap garland around the ladder's top rung. *If and when she's ready.*

From above, she heard the faint sound of Luke banging away at something.

"You're lucky to have him here today," Melody said. "Can you imagine getting a repairman in New York, two days before Christmas?"

"Oh, gosh," Clara replied with a laugh. "The boiler in my apartment building has been acting up and the super says he can't promise a fix before January."

Melody shook her head. "That's the price we pay, isn't it."

"Price?"

"For living in New York. Don't get me wrong: I love the city. It's where I chased my dreams and where my dreams came true." She sighed. "But those dreams came with a price."

Clara was about to probe more when the door to the window display opened and Peggy popped her head in. "Nice," she said, her eyes roving the interior. "I love where you're going with this."

"Thanks," Clara said.

"I'm headed to the cafe for coffee. What can I get you?"

Oh my — coffee! With a jolt, Clara realized she'd had zero caffeine so far that day, a situation in dire need of rectifying. "Thank you, Peggy, I'd love something. A large mocha latte?"

"No prob. Melody, how about you?"

Melody smiled. "Normally, I prefer green tea with a splash of non-sugar sweetener, but...."

"It's almost Christmas," Peggy said. "You're allowed to indulge."

Melody laughed. "You're so right. I would love a hot cocoa."

"Large or small?"

"Small. No, wait — large." She laughed. "Heartsprings Valley is dangerous — very dangerous!"

Peggy smiled. "Does Luke want anything?"

"Let me ask," Clara said. Carefully, she made her way up the tinsel-covered ladder. "Luke, your aunt's doing a coffee run. You want anything?"

He paused and shifted position to look at her. "Small coffee. Black. One sugar."

"Got it."

She repeated his order as she climbed back down.

"Back soon," Peggy said.

"Wait," Clara said. "That's a lot of coffee to carry back. You sure you don't need help?"

"Oh, I'll be fine."

"How about I go with you?" Melody said, then looked at Clara. "Assuming that's okay?"

"Of course," Clara replied. "I'll be good as long as I get my mocha."

"Am I dressed warmly enough?" Melody asked, looking down at her cashmere sweater and pants. "It's getting awfully cold out there."

"You brought a warm jacket, right?" Peggy asked.

"Yes."

"We'll get you bundled up in that. The cafe's across the square, not too far."

Melody turned to Clara. "Back in a bit." She and Peggy left, leaving Clara alone in the window display with the green tinsel ladder-tree. A moment later, the two women appeared outside and waved before heading toward the cafe.

CHAPTER 17

*C*lara returned her attention to the ladder. Green tinsel now covered the entire aluminum structure, which meant it was time for the next step — lighting. She reached down and picked up the bag of colored lights. As she opened the bag, she searched for the window display's electrical outlet and found it in a corner.

Tentatively at first, she wound the string of lights around the legs of the ladder, figuring out as she went along how she wanted to do it. Lighting was always the trickiest part of tree decorating, in her experience. Too many lights and the tree looked over-loaded. Too few, the tree looked forlorn and sad.

Gradually, the right placement emerged and her pace picked up. She'd need at least one more light string, she realized, so she slipped out of the display and headed for the Christmas aisle, which she was quickly becoming very familiar with. She grabbed a second bag of lights. When she returned, Luke was making his way down the ladder.

"First time my ladder's been turned into a tree," he said cheerfully.

Clara smiled. "What's the latest from up north?"

"We're about to find out." He squeezed past her, once again reminding her how tall he was. "The electrical panel's in the storage room, right?"

"Right," she said.

As she watched him go, she realized she was shivering. She'd been so immersed in her tasks, she hadn't realized how downright chilly it was in the display area. If the heat didn't come back soon, she'd be seeing her own breath!

Before she could even finish that thought, Luke was back.

"Fingers crossed," he said as he made his way back up the ladder. She heard him crawl toward the heater. A few seconds later, she heard a soft *whoomph* as the heater turned on.

From the air vent above her, she felt the welcome flow of heated air.

"Hurray!" she said. Excited, she rushed up the ladder and poked her head into the crawlspace. "Luke, you did it."

"Thanks," he said, grinning.

"I can't tell you how much this means to us."

"Happy to help."

"Are you done up here?"

He nodded. "Once I get everything cleaned up. Down in a few."

As she made her way down the ladder, her dad popped his head into the display area. "Heat's back. Luke need anything else?"

Clara shook her head. "He's getting his stuff together and will be down in a few."

"Fantastic," he said, then zipped away. A few seconds later, she heard her dad's voice on the store's speaker system. "Great news, everyone. The heat is back!" She heard a roar of approval from the customers in the store. Her dad continued: "A big round of applause to Luke Matthews of Matthews General Contracting. Great job, Luke." More cheering followed.

Clara couldn't resist running up the ladder one last time. "You hear that?" she asked.

Luke grinned. "Your dad didn't have to do that."

"Of course he did. We were about to turn into popsicles. We really appreciate you doing this."

"Happy to help."

And he *was* happy to help, she realized. Helping others was a cornerstone of the man he'd become. He'd been considerate back in high school, too, but back then he'd been a kid. Now he'd matured, his potential realized. She felt an unexpected rush of emotion, almost like she was going to tear up.

"See you in a few," she said quickly, hurrying

down the ladder before he noticed her response, her feet nearly slipping on the tinsel in her haste.

What was wrong with her today? Why was she suddenly so tongue-tied and unsure? It would be easy to blame her lack of poise on her teenage crush — too easy, she sensed. Which meant something else was going on.

Before she could dig deeper, she heard bangs and bumps above as Luke moved himself and his equipment toward the access hatch. She licked her lips and squared her shoulders to make sure she looked serene and unflappable, then cleared her throat for good measure. His boots appeared, followed by the rest of him, as he carefully carried his toolbox down. He set it on the floor next to the tinseled ladder, then headed back up and pulled the access hatch door shut.

As he made his way down for the final time, he gave her a big grin. His gaze lingered for a long second, his blue eyes alive and intense and focused on her. Then he blinked, as if realizing he was moving into a danger zone.

"Thank you for helping us," she repeated, mentally kicking herself for saying something she'd already said twice.

"Sure," he said, shaking his head as if coming out of a trance. He glanced toward the bag of lights at her feet. "Need help with that?"

"Sure," she replied, grateful for the distraction.

She picked up the bag and opened it. "I'm thinking we should leave a space on each step free of lights in case you need to go back up."

He nodded and started draping. They worked in silence, aware of each other but deliberately keeping their attention on the task at hand. Within just a couple of minutes, the ladder was fully wrapped.

"Does it work?" she asked.

"Let's see." He grabbed the plug and kneeled down and plugged it into the outlet. Instantly, the colorful lights of Christmas filled the space.

"Will you look at that," he said.

"Excellent. Let me pop outside to see how it looks."

She dashed out of the store and onto the sidewalk, sighing in pleasure when she saw how the ladder was transformed. Wrapped in green tinsel and decorated with colorful lights, it really did look like a Christmas tree. Behind it was the outdoor winter vista on the shower curtain, with red curtains on each side. The scene was beginning to look a lot like Christmas.

Luke was awaiting her response, his eyes on her. She gave him a thumb's up and he grinned. He looked as much a part of the tableau as the winter scenery — like he belonged there, surrounded by snow and holiday cheer.

She blinked, realizing she was once again losing herself in unnecessary thoughts. Plus, it was darned cold! She scooted back inside and returned to the display area, which was now warming up quite nicely, thanks to the repaired heater.

"The tree looks great, and so does the backdrop," she said. "But the rest of the room is still looking pretty bare...."

Luke nodded. "I noticed a portable faux fireplace in one of the aisles."

"Will it fit in the corner?"

"It should."

"Good. And I'll get stockings."

He smiled and followed her out. As she returned to the Christmas aisle yet again, she realized she hadn't needed to explain anything to him. The two of them were in sync. She tried to imagine what would happen if they disagreed about something. Two planners, with competing plans? She knew herself well enough to know that she could be pretty stubborn. How stubborn was he? If they kept getting along so well, she'd probably never have to find out.

In the Christmas aisle, she found a set of big red stockings lined with white tufting that looked like upside-down Santa hats. Each stocking had a single word stitched on it in big green lettering. One said "Peace," one said "Joy," and the third said "Noel."

With a smile, she returned to the display window and found Luke already there, positioning the portable fireplace into the corner at an angle.

"That's going to be perfect," she said.

He stepped back to make sure the fireplace was where he wanted it, then bent down and plugged it in. The faux logs began glowing red immediately.

"It's looking nice and cozy in here," she said.

"There's still one important part of the holiday missing," he said.

At the exact same time, they turned to each other and said: "Christmas presents!"

CHAPTER 18

Smiling, without needing to say a word to each other, the two of them made their way out of the window display.

"I'll get empty boxes from the storeroom," he said.

"And I'll get wrapping paper and ribbons and tape," she replied. Once again, she returned to her go-to aisle and considered her options. Her eyes lingered on a roll of deep red paper, rich and luxurious, before wandering to paper depicting a charming winter wonderland of happy snowmen, the white of the snow punctuated with splashes of red and green from the snowmen's winter scarves.

Should she go monochromatic and wrap all of the presents in the same color? If she were back in New York helping one of her clients with his or her holiday decorating, a sleek modern look would be the way to go, without question.

But who was she kidding? Here in Heartsprings Valley, Christmas wouldn't be Christmas without snowmen. And as her gaze traveled over wrapping paper showing jolly Santas and yummy cookies and evergreen wreaths and tree ornaments, she realized it wouldn't be Christmas without all of these other treasured symbols of the season either.

With a laugh, she admitted to herself again how glad she was to be back home. She scooped up a smorgasbord of paper and ribbons and bows, along with tape and scissors, and headed back to the display area.

Luke returned shortly with an assortment of empty boxes from the storeroom. "Do we have enough room in here to do the wrapping?" he asked as he squeezed in.

"I think so," she said. "If we set up on the floor, next to the ladder, we should have enough room, barely." She got down onto her knees. Luke placed an empty box in front of her. She tore the plastic covering off the snowman wrapping paper and unrolled it and draped it over the box.

He surveyed the setup and nodded with approval. "Okay, this will work." He dropped to the ground opposite her, the box between them. "What do you want me to do?"

"How good are you at wrapping presents?"

"Not terrible," he said, "but not an expert."

Which meant he was a typical guy. In all her

years, she had yet to meet a man who truly appreci- ated the finer points of gift-wrapping.

"No worries," she said. "You can start by cutting the paper" — she eyed the paper and the box's proportions — "here."

He picked up the scissors and cleanly sliced the paper. "Like this?"

"Perfect."

He handed her the paper, then picked up the box so that she could slide the paper underneath. She moved the box to the right spot, then began wrap- ping, her movements efficient and practiced.

"You're good at this," he said.

She shrugged. "It's something I picked up as a kid."

"From your mom?"

"That's right."

He didn't reply, and after a few seconds she glanced up from her wrapping to see why. His face told the story: He was aware of something related to her, but he wasn't sure whether Clara knew or how she felt about it.

"I know, by the way," she said.

He blinked. "About?"

"My dad and your aunt. Dating."

"Ah, good."

She pointed to a roll of red ribbon. "If you could get some of that ready."

"Sure." He unspooled the ribbon and picked up the scissors. "How do you feel about that?"

"I'm glad Dad's dating. And your aunt seems very nice."

"Aunt Peg's great. She had a rough go of it the past few years, so it's a relief to see her bouncing back."

"Rough go? What happened?"

He shook his head. "Bad divorce. She found out her husband wasn't faithful." Clara heard the undercurrent of anger in his voice. "The guy was a louse."

"I'm sorry to hear that."

"That was three years ago. About a year ago, my dad — her brother — and my mom convinced her to move here, to give small-town life a try."

"Does she have any kids?"

He shook his head. "She didn't get married until she was in her late thirties. I think she and her husband were trying to get pregnant, but it never took. And when she found out what he was up to…."

Her heart surged with compassion for what Peggy had been through. The woman she'd met today came across as assured and emotionally in a good place. From the sound of it, she'd pushed through a difficult and painful chapter in her life and emerged stronger. Maybe it helped that she now had something important to look forward to: a new romance.

"She told me that she and my dad are moving slowly because they're both a bit ... rusty."

Luke nodded. "Rusty's a good way to describe it. Your dad's a great guy. If there's anyone who can help Aunt Peg trust again...."

While they'd been talking, her hands had been working. The box was now fully covered with happy snowmen.

"Ribbon time," she said. He handed her the ribbon, and with a few expert loops, the present was wrapped. "Scissors," she said. He picked up the scissors and sliced off the unneeded bit. "Tape." He tore off a strip and, while she held the ribbon in place, watched him apply the tape to the end of the ribbon.

"One thing more."

"Red bow?" he asked with a smile.

"Exactly," she said, smiling back.

He handed her a big red bow and she taped it firmly in place, then picked up the box and examined it from every angle.

"Does it get the Clara Cane stamp of approval?" he asked, a gleam in his eye.

"I should hope so."

"How about her wrapping assistant? How did he do?"

She laughed. "He did just fine."

"Good."

She was about to say more when she heard a tap

on the glass. Peggy and Melody were grinning at them through the window, their arms loaded with coffees and treats.

Clara's heart leaped.

Caffeine!

CHAPTER 19

*H*ow could she have gone the entire day without a single drop of coffee? The thought was practically inconceivable. Perhaps her mocha-free state explained why she'd felt so off-balance today. Maybe all she needed to restore her equilibrium was a jolt of caffeinated goodness.

She realized Luke was watching her — with amusement. "You really need that latte, don't you?" he said.

"You have no idea," she said fervently. She stood up, slipped past her wrapping partner, pushed open the door to the display area, and rushed toward Peg and Melody, who had made their way inside the store.

Peg saw the look on Clara's face and laughed as she handed Clara her drink. "A fellow addict?"

"Big-time," Clara said as she accepted the latte. "Thank you so much." She nearly gasped aloud at the welcome heat in her hands. She raised the cup to her nose and inhaled the delightful aroma. With a grateful sigh, she brought the cup to her lips. Oh, this was heaven. The wonderful taste, soothing and rich, brought her taste buds to life. Sometimes it was the simple pleasures that made all the difference.

Next to Peg, Melody was also warming her hands with her drink.

"Glad you chose the hot cocoa?" Clara asked after letting the mocha linger on her tongue.

Melody chuckled. "I feel so decadent."

Peg raised her eyes toward the heating vents in the ceiling. "Is that hot air I feel?"

"Yep," Clara said.

"Hooray!"

At that moment, Luke joined them.

"Luke, thank you," Peg said as she handed him his coffee. "You have no idea how much this means to us. You are the best nephew ever."

He grinned. "Happy to help."

Melody said, "I see you two've made progress with the window display."

Clara nodded. "It's coming along great. It was Luke's idea to add the fireplace."

Peg's eyes darted between Clara and Luke. "It's good to see you two catching up."

"We're having fun," Luke agreed.

"Totally," Clara added.

There was an awkward pause as everyone tried to figure out what to say next. Melody broke the silence by turning to Clara. "Darling, do you remember I mentioned the bookstore? I simply must pop in there and peruse the offerings. When I think of myself in my lovely room at the Inn, I simply can't imagine not having a good book to curl up with."

"Peruse away," Clara said. "I'll be here for a while — I still have some work to do with the window display."

"You sure you don't need my help?"

"I'll be fine."

"I can stay and help out," Luke threw in.

Clara felt a rush of pleasure. "You sure?"

"Of course," he said, turning his gaze toward her. "There's no place I'd rather be."

She felt her face go pink as his words sank in. "Great," she said brightly, in a tone that she hoped conveyed cheerful efficiency.

"Perfect," Peg added with a smile. "I'll leave you two kids to it."

Suddenly, Melody and Peg were gone, and it was back to just her and Luke.

Her window-display partner took a sip from his coffee and waited for her to speak. Clara followed his lead and took another big sip from her latte.

"It's nice to have a moment of quiet every now and then," he said.

"Agreed."

"Though I like it better when I'm busy."

"Me, too."

"Busy's good."

"Agreed."

There was another silence, this one less awkward but still noticeable, as each waited for the other to make the next move.

"You like living here?" she asked.

He nodded. "I do."

"Even after everything you experienced out in the big wide world?"

"Even more so." When he saw her raised eyebrows, he continued. "Being away all these years helped me appreciate what I left behind. It's easy to take things for granted, especially when you're younger."

He was right about that. "I can relate."

"Don't get me wrong — I'm glad I saw what I saw, and glad I was part of what I was part of. I'll always be grateful for those experiences."

"But out there wasn't where you needed to be."

"That's right."

There was another pause, then she said, "Let's get that display finished."

He smiled and stepped aside. "After you."

The wrapping went quickly with the two of them working as a team. Without needing to talk about it, they settled into a system: He cut the paper, she wrapped the box, he got the tape and ribbons and bows prepped, and she applied the finishing touches. Before they knew it, Christmas gifts surrounded them.

"Think we have enough?" he asked as he looked at the giant stack of gifts waiting to be arranged around the Christmas tree.

"I think so," she said. "Maybe too many?"

"No such thing." He pointed to the tree. "Ornaments?"

"Absolutely."

He stood up and she followed suit.

"For the top," she said. "I'm thinking a …."

"Star?"

She grinned. "Exactly." As she slipped past him, her hand brushed his and she felt the same electric jolt as before. Her heart thumped in her chest and her breath caught.

Stay focused, she told herself as she made her way to the decorations aisle. Yes, she was enjoying decorating with him. But decorating was the *only thing* going on. Nothing less, and *nothing more*. Sure, they were getting along well, but so what? She got along well with lots of people. And so what if their ideas about what to do seemed so well synced? All they'd really done was agree about stuff they happened to agree about.

Don't try to deny what's really going on here, a rebellious voice whispered before she could quash it. Resolutely, she turned her attention to the ornaments in the aisle and the task at hand. At the top of a shelf, just within reach of her fingertips, was the perfect star for the top of the tree: five points, painted a bright silver to catch reflected light, not too small and not too large. With difficulty, she eased it off the shelf and into her waiting hand. She selected three boxes of ornaments and a container of fasteners as well.

When she got back to Luke, she squeezed past him and handed him the star ornament.

"Me?" he said, surprised.

"Please."

She stepped back and watched him carefully climb the ladder and affix the star to the top of the tree.

"How's it look?" he asked.

"Perfect."

She opened the first of the three ornament boxes, which contained six shiny globes of different colors. After placing the ornaments on the tree, she opened the second box, which contained different Nutcracker figurines. The last box held a dozen different ornaments of various Christmas figures: Santa Claus, Rudolph the red-nosed reindeer, brightly colored candy canes, red stockings stuffed with toys, beautifully wrapped holiday gifts, and — of course! — a trio of jolly snowmen.

After hanging them on the tree, they stood back to admire their handiwork.

"Best-looking ladder I've ever seen," he said.

She laughed. "Not bad for a rush job." She gestured toward the stack of Christmas gifts. "Last step, and I think we're done."

He nodded, then gestured toward the sidewalk. "We have an audience."

She turned and saw her dad, Peggy, and Melody in front of the hardware store, watching them. Melody gave her a smile and a thumb's up. Peggy said something, and her dad and Melody nodded.

"I wonder what they're talking about?" she said.

"Up to no good, I bet," Luke said with a grin.

Quickly, they arranged the boxes around the tree into a pleasing display.

"We done?" he asked.

After a final glance around, she nodded. "Let's see what it looks like from outside."

Together, they made their way to the sidewalk and joined the others.

When she turned to look at their creation, she let out a small gasp. The hardware store's window display had been transformed into a Christmas tableau bursting with warmth and holiday cheer. The ladder, wrapped in green tinsel and dotted with multicolored lights and ornaments, almost looked like a real tree. The faux fireplace cast a cozy red glow over the pile of beautifully wrapped gifts nestled around the tree. Against the backdrop of the snow-covered landscape framed by rich red curtains, the room beckoned with its embrace of the season's blessings.

Melody put an arm around Clara's shoulders and squeezed. "You did it, darling."

"*We* did it," Clara said. "A real team effort."

"Agreed."

Clara turned to her dad. "What do you think?"

"Looks terrific!" her dad said, beaming.

Peggy added, "We owe you and Melody and Luke such a big thanks for helping out today."

There was a long pause, and then her dad said, "Say, um, honey, about tomorrow."

"Yes, Dad?"

"I realized, um, how busy we're going to be at the store," he said, uncharacteristically stumbling over his words. "So I had an idea."

"You had an idea?" she said, deliberately keeping her tone of voice neutral. She knew her dad well enough to know that the idea about to pop out of his mouth wasn't really his — the idea was Peggy's or Melody's, and they had put him up to it. Truly, he was a terrible liar. But for the moment, her curiosity won out over her wariness.

"Um, yeah, an idea. Since we're going to be so

busy tomorrow, we're going to need Peggy here at the store."

"Okay," she said, still not seeing where this was going.

"So for the cookie contest, how about you and Luke partner up instead?"

CHAPTER 20

*C*lara's eyes widened in shock. *What?*

Next to her, she heard Luke breathe in sharply.

Before either of them could reply, Peggy jumped in. "It would be such a huge help if you could do this," she said to both of them. "The store will be so busy tomorrow — all that last-minute shopping."

"Completely insane," Melody purred in agreement, her eyes wide and solemn. "Utter madness."

Clara almost laughed — how would Melody know that? — but somehow she managed to maintain her composure and, just barely, her silence. Clearly the meddling gene ran deep in this town. Even worse, it had somehow turned into a highly contagious virus. Everyone was infected.

Her dad was watching her closely, trying to read her eyes and mouth for hints at her reaction.

He switched his attention to Luke and she followed. Her window-decorating partner was staring at his aunt with a mixture of exasperation and — did she catch a hint of something else as well?

"Aunt Peg," Luke said, then stopped, seemingly at a loss for words.

Was Luke's response the same as hers? Was he simultaneously annoyed and…?

Clara blinked as she realized that the possibility of entering the contest with Luke did more than irritate her. It unsettled her. And that was because, truth be told….

The idea *excited* her.

Gah!

Next to her, Luke remained silent, but she noted a touch of color on his cheeks.

"I'm sure," Peg said smoothly, "that between the two of you, you can come up with a contest-winning cookie."

Luke's gaze swung from his aunt toward Clara. She blinked at the force of his blazing blue eyes as he scanned her face for clues to how she felt about the meddling maneuver now under way.

Whatever he saw seemed to make up his mind. Squaring his shoulders, his voice deep and gruff but with a hint of hopefulness, he said, "I'm game if you are."

The rush of excitement took her by surprise, but

she managed to say, in a tone that pleased her with its calmness, "Sure, that sounds like fun."

Needing to direct her upsurge of emotion somewhere, she whirled on the trio of meddlers. "And for the record, we know what you three are up to."

The trio immediately adopted expressions of baffled innocence.

"What do you mean, honey?" her dad said, very unconvincingly.

"Dad, we grew up here," Clara replied, not giving an inch. "We know all of this town's tricks."

"Every single one of them," Luke added.

"Now, having said that," Clara said, "I happen to think the cookie contest will be fun."

"And I happen to agree," Luke said.

"I think we'll make a great team."

"Agreed."

"Both of us love competing."

"Absolutely."

"And we love to win."

"You bet."

"And I know the perfect recipe."

"Wait a sec."

Startled, she turned and found her new baking partner looking at her with a mixture of surprise and anxiety.

He swallowed, then said, "My grandma made the best sugar cookies ever. With her recipe, we can't lose."

Now it was her turn to inhale sharply. Was this going to be their first disagreement? She took another deep breath, willing herself to proceed cautiously. "I'm sure your grandmother's recipe is wonderful, but my mom's sugar cookie recipe is out-of-this-world delicious. I know that if we use her recipe, we'll win without question."

They stared at each other, both at a loss for words. Even as the rational side of her brain frantically tried to remind her that the cookie contest was something she'd barely cared about a few minutes ago, and that the cookies themselves didn't matter because winning wasn't the point of entering, the emotional part of her brain was rising up to defend the honor of her mother's truly amazing recipe for sugar cookies. Her stubborn streak was beginning to assert itself.

Compounding the problem: She sensed a similar process happening within Luke. They were both planners, after all, and instinctive defenders of family tradition. Usually when it came to competing plans, there was room for compromise or negotiation. But no such wiggle room existed when it came to baking. Baking required precision. If two recipes were in conflict, only one could win.

Lost in thought, searching desperately for a way to get herself and Luke on the same page, she heard Melody say, "Darling, I know just what to do."

"Oh, you do?" Clara said, not holding out much hope.

"We'll have a cookie audition."

Clara went still as she let the idea sink in, then swiveled to give her full attention to the Broadway star. "Say that again?"

Melody was beaming. "An audition. You can each audition your recipe."

"Meaning a … bake-off?"

"Yes, exactly! Each of you can bake up a batch of your cookies before the contest. Then we'll do a blind taste test."

"I love this idea," Peg said quickly.

"Sounds terrific," her dad added immediately.

Clara found herself inclined to agree — a bake-off sounded both workable and fair. "When?" she said, her mind immediately gravitating toward the practicalities.

"Tomorrow morning?" Melody asked.

"Where?"

"Our kitchen," her dad volunteered.

"Who will be the judges?"

"Me," Melody said promptly. "And I'll ask Barbara and Stu to join."

Clara took a deep breath, then turned to Luke. "Well, partner?"

He nodded approvingly. "Sounds like a plan."

"Agreed," Clara said.

Luke grinned at her, a teasing look in his eyes. "Glad we're back to agreeing. But a word of warning — I don't hold back, and neither did my grandma.

Her cookies are incredible. I'd love to win a cookie contest with her recipe — it'd be great to add that victory to my trophy case."

She grinned back. "You're not the only one who likes to win. And my mom's cookies are amazing. Bring it on, mister."

He chuckled. "Careful what you wish for, Ms. Clara Cane. I aim to win. Game *on*."

CHAPTER 21

a gust of arctic air reminded everyone they were standing outside in the freezing cold. The merry meddlers, satisfied that they'd achieved their goal, announced they had things to do and places to be. Peggy and her dad scooted back inside the store. Luke followed them to collect his toolbox.

Clara turned to Melody. "How about we head to the chocolate shop so I can introduce you to Abby?"

"Perfect," Melody replied.

Luke returned with his toolkit and paused before heading to his truck. "I'll see you tomorrow morning," he said. She sensed he would have said more if Melody hadn't been there. "You guys should get inside. It's getting really cold out here."

"We're headed to Abby's," Clara said.

He nodded. "See you tomorrow." With a final glance over his shoulder, he walked across the street to his truck, hopped in, and started the engine. He gave them a wave as he pulled away, his eyes lingering on Clara.

Clara felt Melody grab her arm. She turned, startled.

"Darling," Melody breathed. "He's so dreamy."

"Stop it," Clara said, feeling her cheeks flame red as she struggled out of Melody's grasp.

"I think he likes you."

"Stop it," she said more forcefully, even as Melody's words caused an uncontrollable flareup of excitement.

Her client broke into a rich, melodious laugh. "Fine, I'll stop."

"Will you? Really?"

Melody gave her a teasing smile. "For now."

"Thank you." Clara took a deep breath, willing her heart to stop beating so fast. "Let's focus instead on something real. Like chocolate."

"Mmm, I love chocolate. Though if you're suggesting that what's going on between you and Luke isn't real, you're in denial."

"Melody," Clara said warningly.

"Or crazy."

"Melody, I'm serious. Chocolate. Let's focus on chocolate."

"Whatever you say," her client said, the teasing tone still in her voice. "Whatever you say."

Clara very firmly took hold of Melody's arm and

guided her down the sidewalk toward Abby's Chocolate Heaven.

"You know," Melody said as they walked, "pairing up you and Luke for the cookie contest wasn't your dad's idea."

"Yes, I know that."

"Peggy and I thought it up."

"Yes, I know that, too."

"You'll thank us later."

When they reached the store, Clara took hold of Melody by the shoulders and looked her straight in the eye. "Chocolate. When we walk in there, we're going to focus on chocolate, okay?"

"Fine," her client said. "Chocolate it is."

"Good." With that fragile promise in hand, Clara pushed open the door to Abby's Chocolate Heaven and was immediately enveloped in the welcoming aroma of cocoa and spices. The heady warmth embraced her. As always during the holiday season, the store was decorated with garlands of holly covered in white lights and Christmas ornaments.

Behind the counter, a woman with a kind face and brown hair, shoulder-length and flecked with gray, lit up when she saw Clara walk in. "Clara, so good to see you." She rushed from around the counter to give Clara a big hug. Beneath the woman's white apron, a red holiday sweater showed a reindeer with a familiar red nose.

"Abby!" Clara said as she was pulled into the friendly embrace. "Merry Christmas."

Abby let her go, then turned toward Melody and stuck out her hand. "Ms. Connelly, I'm Abby, owner of this little store and a huge fan. I saw *London, Here I Come!* this summer and loved your performance."

"Thank you so much," Melody said, taking Abby's hand in hers. "Such a pleasure to meet you. I'm so glad you enjoyed the show."

"Oh, we had so much fun. Such a memorable night at the theater. The humor and the songs and the emotion were wonderful."

"That's so kind of you to say."

"And now to have you here, in my little shop." Abby looked around in disbelief. "Pinch me — I must be dreaming."

Melody laughed. "Your shop is adorable — and smells so delicious. I understand you make your chocolates here?"

Abby nodded. "In the back. The space is tiny, but I make it work."

Clara stepped closer to the display counter to feast her eyes on the delights inside. Rows of gorgeous truffles were there to tempt her — bite-size morsels of dark chocolate, hazelnut, almond, raspberry, lemon, and more — along with nougats and caramels and brittles.

"Abby," Clara said, her stomach rumbling in anticipation, "you know I won't be able to leave here without loading up."

Abby laughed. "If I remember right, you're partial to the nougats."

"Completely, totally helpless. And also weak for truffles."

"Ah, yes, truffles."

With difficulty, Clara tore her gaze from the delectable display. "Before we dive into the very important business of picking the perfect dozen chocolates for me, let's talk about tomorrow. You sure it's okay to do a chocolate-making session here tomorrow afternoon?"

"Of course. My neighbor's daughter Ava agreed to help out at the counter to make sure we aren't disturbed in back." With a glance at Melody, she added, "I was thinking we could make a batch of chocolate truffles."

"Lovely. You're the expert — whatever you believe is best."

"Excellent," Clara said. "The way it works is, we'll shoot video while you two make chocolates. When Melody gets back to New York, we'll edit the footage and post it on her social media to share with her followers."

"That sounds wonderful," Abby said, then turned to Melody. "I hear you're thinking about hosting a cooking show."

"That's right," Melody said.

Clara said, "You heard that? Who from?"

"Gosh, I'm not sure," Abby said, very vaguely. "You know, I also heard that Luke Matthews helped out today at the hardware store — fixing the heating system and pitching in to help with the window display. He's such a nice young man."

Clara sighed. Abby was much more skilled at meddling than her dad was. Her technique was indirect rather than straight-ahead — designed to prompt further conversation.

"No," Clara said.

Abby blinked. "No?"

"No, we are not going to talk about Luke Matthews."

Melody laughed out loud, and Abby smiled and said, "I hope you don't blame me for trying. He really has grown up to be a wonderful young man."

"Indeed he has," Clara said, "but we're here to talk about *chocolates*. Speaking of which, I'd like a dozen, please. Six nougats and six truffles, your choice."

"Same for me," Melody piped up.

"All right, I can take a hint," Abby said with a grin. "Two dozen chocolates, as requested. And no talk of handsome available men."

CHAPTER 22

Fifteen minutes later, with the chocolate-making session arranged and a box of delectable treats tucked under her arm, Clara walked with Melody back to the Inn, snow crunching beneath her boots and frigid air whipping across her cheeks. The air smelled fresh and crisp — so unlike what she was used to in the big city. The moon was rising, its pale white light reflecting on the snow blanketing the tree branches and front yards.

"Would you like to get dinner later?" Clara asked as they approached the Inn.

"Oh, darling, thank you," Melody said, "but Barbara said she was whipping up something for the guests. And to be completely honest, I'm knackered. Such a busy day."

"No worries," Clara said, relieved by her client's answer. "I'll see you in the morning?"

"Of course." Melody reached out and pulled Clara in for a big hug. "You've been such a dear today. I know I can be a bother sometimes. I truly appreciate everything you do."

Once again, Clara found herself battling unexpected tears. Her client sounded so sincere — almost like the day had been an escape for her. "I'm glad to help."

Melody stepped back to look Clara in the face. "Now, about the bake-off. You seem awfully confident about your mother's recipe."

"I'm confident because I truly believe her recipe is the best."

"Do I detect a gleam in your eye?"

Clara grinned. "Let's just say a certain secret ingredient is required."

"Aha. A secret ingredient. No chance you'll go easy on Luke and give him a fighting shot?"

"Not a chance."

"Good girl. See you tomorrow."

She watched Melody make her way into the Inn, then turned and walked the two blocks home. Her client's true motive for rushing here before Christmas remained a mystery, but at least she'd gotten her settled at the Inn and provided her lots of small-town video moments. Even amidst the craziness of this very crazy day, she'd managed to do a good job for her client.

As she pushed open the front door of her childhood home, a wave of weariness hit her. How silly she'd been this morning, believing she might actually find rest and relaxation at home for Christmas. The day had been a nonstop rush from the moment her alarm had yanked her from sleep at 6:23 a.m.

Sadly, the rush wasn't over. Thanks to the cookie contest, she now had one more errand. She pulled open the top-right drawer of the entryway sideboard, grabbed the town phone book, flipped to the name she was looking for, and used her phone to punch in the numbers. On the third ring, a familiar voice picked up.

"Hello?" a man said, his voice hearty and raspy.

"Mr. Merrigold? It's Clara Cane."

"Clara! So good to hear your voice. How are you?"

"I'm great. I just got back to town today."

"Home for Christmas with your dad."

"That's right."

"Good, good — so glad you're back. We think about you often, Jo and I, wondering how you're doing down there in New York."

"I'm doing great. But it's good to be home."

He chuckled. "I bet I can guess why you're calling."

Clara smiled. "You can?"

"We have some set aside just for you."

She exhaled with relief. "Thank you so much. Would it be okay if I head over right now?"

"We'll be waiting."

"See you in a bit, Mr. Merrigold. Thank you so much."

A smile still on her face, she picked up the keys to her dad's car and made her way to the garage. With the press of a button on the keychain, the garage door cranked up, revealing an all-wheel-drive car inside. With the press of another button, the car unlocked itself.

Quickly, she hopped inside and pressed the start button. After a second of protesting, the car came to life. While the engine warmed, she adjusted the seat and side mirrors — she and her dad were very different sizes — and turned on the radio, changing it from the sports talk station to the town's local radio station. As the sound of Bing Crosby's velvety voice filled the car, she exhaled with relief and settled in, singing along with Bing as she adjusted the hot air vents so that the flow of heat was aimed away from her face. With a contented sigh, she put the car in reverse and backed out, then shifted the car into all-wheel-drive and headed out.

On either side of her, houses were festooned with all manner of holiday lights and yard displays. She smiled and sang louder. Her voice was no match for Bing's, of course, but she gave it her all anyway.

The gaps between houses grew wider as she left her neighborhood and headed out of town. She began passing farms and small businesses as she drove further into the valley.

A new song — "It's Beginning to Look a Lot Like Christmas" — followed Bing's, and she happily sang along as she kept her eyes peeled for the road she knew was coming up. When her headlights caught the road sign for Merrigold Way, she tapped the brakes, signaled her turn, and carefully pulled off the main road. Paying close attention, she aimed down a winding road barely wide enough for her car. Wooden fencing pressed close on both sides, the posts topped with caps of fresh snow. The night seemed darker out here, the car headlights offering the only illumination.

Up ahead, a twinkle of lights — from inside the windows of a farmhouse — grew brighter as she approached. In one of the windows, she saw a curtain being pulled back and a figure peering out. Behind the figure, she spied a Christmas tree covered with lights.

She pulled into the farm's driveway and parked behind a big truck. With a tingle of anticipation, she hopped out and made her way to the front porch, stamping her boots on the doormat to shake off the snow.

As she was about to knock, the door swung open and a bespectacled man of medium height appeared. He was around sixty, with a round face, bushy mustache, and mostly bald head, dressed in coveralls and a blue plaid flannel shirt.

"Mr. Merrigold," Clara said. "Merry Christmas."

Mr. Merrigold let out a happy chuckle and pulled the door wide open. "Merry Christmas to you, too. Come on in."

As she stepped inside, a woman bustled up, wiping her hands on her apron. "Clara, dear. Merry Christmas." She pulled Clara in for a hug. "Welcome home."

"Thank you, Mrs. Merrigold," Clara said. "I'm really glad to be back. It's so good to see both of you."

"It's been too long, dear," Mrs. Merrigold said, then let her go. Around the same age as her husband, she was a thin woman with warm brown eyes and a wide, welcoming smile. Underneath her apron, she was dressed in comfortable jeans and a blue-and-gold wool sweater. Her shoulder-length gray hair was pulled back into a ponytail, perhaps to keep it out of the way of whatever she was whipping up in the kitchen.

Speaking of which…. The lovely aroma of honey-roasted ham wafted toward them. "My apologies for interrupting your dinner."

"Nonsense, dear," Mrs. Merrigold said. "We're thrilled to see you. How's New York treating you?"

"It's great. The job's keeping me busy. How are you? How's the farm?"

"Oh, we're doing fine," Mrs. Merrigold said. "Scaling back a bit — these old bones are getting a bit creaky — but still at it."

Her husband added, "The gals are doing great."

Clara smiled. She knew the gals well — tending to them had been one of her part-time jobs back in high school. "How's Geraldine?"

"Geraldine's doing great. She'll be happy to see you."

Mrs. Merrigold examined her closely. From the look on her face, she wasn't completely pleased. "Would you like something to eat, dear? You look like you could use it."

"Thanks, but no. I'll be heading home to have dinner with Dad."

"You got something started?"

"No, but no worries. Dad and I will figure something out."

Mrs. Merrigold shook her head. "New York City is running you ragged. You need some rest and recuperation."

"I'm fine," Clara said, a bit alarmed that her appearance might be cause for worry. How tired did she really look?

"I know you're a good cook, dear, just like your mother, but I don't like the idea of you having to put together a meal from scratch, not after the day you just had. And you know that father of yours can't cook to save his life." She shook her head. "No, I'll put together something for the two of you to enjoy."

Clara was torn between feeling grateful and feeling worried, and — wait, what had Mrs.

Merrigold said? She cleared her throat. "Um, the day I just had?"

Mrs. Merrigold sighed. "Yes, dear. Everyone demanding every minute of your time. All that work. You need rest."

All true. But still…. "How do you know I've been so busy?"

With a snort, Mr. Merrigold pointed to the phone. "How else? Darn thing's been ringing all day."

"Now, George," Mrs. Merrigold said, releasing Clara and swiveling toward her husband to protest.

"Don't you 'George' me. The Heartsprings Valley Instant News Network is alive and kicking. That's all I'm going to say." Then he added, "You and Luke can figure out your own lives. The way I see it, the last thing you kids need is well-intentioned folks getting into your business."

Clara couldn't help herself — she laughed. "Thank you. I'll be fine. And Mrs. Merrigold, yes, please, I'm sure Dad would love something to bring home. The aroma from the kitchen is wonderful."

Mrs. Merrigold beamed. "You could do with a bit of meat on your bones. And your dad works too hard. You take after him, you know — both of you, always busy busy busy."

Mr. Merrigold rubbed his hands together. "How about we head to the barn while Jo gets something together for you and your dad?"

"Sounds great," Clara said. "After you."

CHAPTER 23

*M*r. Merrigold led Clara through the living room — a warm, comfortable space with a big blue couch and a leather lounge chair facing a brightly lit Christmas tree — and into the kitchen. On the burner, two pots were gently warming. In the oven, Clara could tell by the delightful aroma, a honeyed ham was approaching cooked perfection.

Mr. Merrigold opened the kitchen's back door and stepped outside, holding it as Clara followed. "Cold one tonight."

Clara shivered as frigid air hit her face. "You're not kidding."

"I imagine it gets pretty cold down in New York, too."

"It can. Especially around now and into January."

She followed him toward a barn across the

driveway from the house. Nearly three stories high, with the Merrigold Farms logo painted above the big doors, the barn dwarfed the farmhouse. Mr. Merrigold pulled open a big, heavy door and ushered her inside. Immediately, the temperature rose and the smells of animals and cut hay filled her nostrils. She smiled as her eyes wandered over familiar wooden beams and stalls. As a teenager, she'd worked in this barn for an hour every morning for two years, helping the Merrigolds with their chores. She knew every inch of this space. She missed it, she realized — a lot.

Without another word, she walked up to the third stall on the left and peered in at a beautiful black-and-white Jersey cow whose gentle face and eyes were intimately familiar to her. She'd witnessed this cow's birth and watched her grow up. Of all the cows in the Merrigold herd, this lovely gal held a special place in her heart.

"Hey, Geraldine," she said softly.

Geraldine blinked. With a quickness that surprised those who didn't know much about cows, she dashed up to Clara, her sensitive nose quivering with excitement. She mooed softly and nuzzled Clara's face.

Clara laughed and took Geraldine's head in her hands as the cow's nose pressed into her cheek. "So good to see you, girl."

Geraldine mooed in agreement, then turned to

look behind her at a calf shyly approaching.

"Who is this?" Clara exclaimed.

"That," Mr. Merrigold said, "is Ariel, our newest addition. Geraldine gave birth to her a few weeks ago."

Ariel approached the stall fence and cautiously sniffed at Clara's leg.

"Ariel is such a nice name."

"Our granddaughter named her, after a princess in one of her favorite movies."

Ariel sniffed again and, inspired by her mother's example, stuck her nose through the wooden slats of the stall and against Clara's leg.

"You are so adorable," Clara said, bending down to give Ariel's cheek a caress.

"The herd's up to fourteen now," Mr. Merrigold said. "A full house."

Clara gestured toward the other stalls. "Is Ellie still around?"

"Sadly, no. She passed this summer."

"I'm sorry to hear that," Clara replied, her mind bringing forth fond memories of the matriarch of the Merrigolds' herd. "How old was she?"

"Twenty-two. She went quickly, which was a relief." There was a pause as Mr. Merrigold cleared his throat. "Her last day was with her herd, out in the pasture. When we woke up the next morning, we found her in her stall."

"She lived a long and happy life. You and Mrs. Merrigold took such good care of her."

"We did our best. Let's get you what you came for."

Clara didn't move — little Ariel was still nuzzling her — but she watched Mr. Merrigold walk to a big refrigerator in the back of the barn, open the door, and grab two big jars of bright yellow butter.

Involuntarily, her mouth started to water. Inside those jars was something almost magical — some of the finest small-batch cultured butter in all of New England. With a higher fat content than most butter (86 percent versus 80 percent), Merrigold Farms butter was ideal for baking, with a creamy, rich, tangy, nutty flavor and a perfect amount of salt. Cookies with Merrigold butter were crispier around the edges, crumblier in the center, and deliciously buttery in taste.

As a secret baking weapon, the butter was to-die-for. Luke Matthews didn't stand a chance.

"I can almost taste it now," Clara said as Mr. Merrigold returned to her, a jar in each hand. "Your butter — there's nothing like it."

"Thank you, dear. But give credit where credit is due."

She turned back to Geraldine and reached out to pull the cow's head closer. "Thank you, Geraldine, for your delicious high-fat milk. It is so good to see you, and to meet your daughter." Geraldine nuzzled her again and gently mooed, as if telling her to come back soon.

Reluctantly, her hand lingering on Geraldine's cheek, Clara turned to her host. "She is such a sweetheart."

"You ready?"

"Not really," she said, then sighed and tore herself away. "But duty calls. You want me to take those jars?"

"I'm good."

Together, they walked to the barn door. Clara pushed the door open and, after Mr. Merrigold stepped past her, she turned around and pushed the door shut.

They made their way back into the farmhouse. Mrs. Merrigold glanced up from the counter, where she was sealing a plastic container. "I've got honeyed ham, mashed potatoes, and green beans for you and your dad."

"You did *not* have to do this," Clara said gratefully. "But I'm glad you did."

Mr. Merrigold picked out a brown shopping bag and carefully placed the butter jars and plastic food containers inside.

"Here you go, Clara. Merry Christmas."

Clara looked with fondness at the couple in front of her. Once again, tears threatened. She was so lucky to know these wonderful people.

"Thank you both so much, for everything that you do," she said. "Merry Christmas!"

CHAPTER 24

*W*ith her precious cargo stowed on the front passenger seat beside her, Clara started up the car. Engine rumbling, she headed back down Merrigold Way toward the main road, her headlights illuminating the tracks she'd made through the snow just minutes before. From hard-won experience, she knew the narrow lane was prone to icy buildup, so she drove slowly, hoping her all-wheel-drive had sufficient traction to get her down the lane without incident.

Two tense minutes later, with a sigh of relief, she reached the main road. As she turned left and headed home, the radio started playing one of her all-time Christmas favorites. At the top of her lungs, her spirits soaring, she joined along, singing loudly about chestnuts and open fires.

If only Christmas could last the entire year. Even

as that wonderful thought danced through her head, a competing thought intruded: What if it did? Would Christmas still have the same magic if it happened, say, on a sweltering summer day in New York City, when the air hung hot and dense, when the city's asphalt and steel pulsed with heat, when even a walk to the corner deli became a test of endurance? Would she have the same cozy, warm feelings about Christmas if her favorite holiday happened on a day when even the simple act of breathing was a chore?

The thought wasn't a happy one. Something about the scenario she'd just imagined didn't sit right. The Christmas part of the idea wasn't what was bothering her. Something else was bubbling up.

Before she could probe further, she noticed, in the bright beam of the headlights, snowflakes beginning to fall. She hadn't checked the weather forecast today, but her gut told her that Heartsprings Valley was about to get a light dusting — enough to cover everything with a fresh coat of white. Nothing to worry about, in other words, as she made her way home.

Very firmly, she decided that now was *not* the time to dig deeper into what might be swirling around inside her. Instead, she dove headlong into the happiness bubbling up as she really, truly embraced the fact that she was *home for Christmas*. Through the light snowfall, she gazed with pleasure at homes decorated with dazzling displays of bright holiday lights. So many of her neighbors had gone all-out to turn their homes and front yards and trees into nighttime tributes to the joy of the season. In Heartsprings Valley, the spirit of Christmas burned bright and strong.

Instead of driving straight home, she swung by the main square, slowing as she passed the hardware store. The window display — the Christmas tree surrounded by wrapped presents, next to the roaring fire, the rich red curtains framing the winter wonderland outside — really did look lovely. It was amazing what a little bit of work could accomplish.

The store was closed for the night, which meant her dad was either on his way home or already there. She turned off the square and made her way the last few blocks home. Occasionally, through the windows in the homes she passed, she caught sight of folks moving about inside.

A few moments later, she pulled into the driveway of her childhood home, punched the garage opener on the dashboard, watched the door creak open, and carefully inched the car in. With the Merrigolds' bounty in her arms, she stepped out and made her way inside.

As she closed the front door behind her, she heard the sound of a cabinet shutting in the kitchen.

"Dad, I'm home," she said as she placed the bag on the sideboard in the front hall and shrugged out of her winter coat.

Her dad popped his head out from the kitchen. "I was looking at what we can rustle up for dinner."

"The Merrigolds made something for us."

"Did they now?" He scooted up to the sideboard and peeked inside the bag. "Is that Jo's famous honeyed ham?"

"Sure is," she said as she unwrapped her scarf and hung it over her coat.

"This is great. I'm starving. But first things first." He motioned to her. "Give your dad a hug."

She stepped toward him and smiled as his big strong arms enveloped her.

"Merry Christmas, Dad," she said, her cheek pressed into his shoulder.

"Merry Christmas, Clara," he said, his voice soft in her ear. "I'm so glad you're here. It's so good to see my little girl."

He stepped back and held her at arm's length so that he could give her a long and loving look, then let her go and picked up the bag. "Let's eat."

"Perfect."

They made their way into the kitchen and, without having to say a word, began setting the small dining table. The kitchen wasn't large, but it was comfortable and well-designed, with creamy-white cabinets and gray marble countertops in a galley-style layout that opened onto the small table in the back next to the bay windows. Fifteen years earlier, her mom had masterminded a thorough renovation to maximize storage and counter space. The space still worked well, though the cabinets needed a fresh coat of paint and the old fridge, dishwasher, and oven were long overdue for replacement.

Her dad, who was unpacking the bag on the counter, pulled out a jar of the Merrigold butter. "So that's why you went out there."

"You bet."

"You say hi to Geraldine?"

"Of course. And her newborn calf."

He smiled as he gathered plates and forks and knives from various drawers. From different drawers, Clara grabbed two placemats and two napkins and set them on the table, then got two drinking glasses and filled them with water from the sink. She watched as he finished arranging everything, then brought the water to the table and set the glasses down.

He grabbed the containers of food from the counter while Clara got serving forks and spoons.

"We forget anything?" he asked.

She smiled and shook her head. The two of them had followed the exact same routine since her mom had died; he took care of the plates and utensils, she handled the water and placemats and napkins, and he said "We forget anything?" before sitting down. There was something so comforting, so reassuring, about the familiar ritual.

With a contented sigh, her dad picked up a fork and dug into the mashed potatoes.

"Mmm," he murmured, his mouth full. "So good."

She followed suit, letting the creamy warmth and smoothness envelope her tongue. Mrs. Merrigold made her mashed potatoes with a touch of garlic, a dollop of heavy cream and an even bigger dollop of her farm's special butter. The resulting taste — rich and tangy and utterly delicious — was one that Clara treasured.

"How's that boss of yours?" her dad asked between mouthfuls.

"Good. He's with Pamela and the kids in the Caribbean."

"Does that mean he's out of your hair for a few days?"

"Knowing him, I doubt it. I'm hoping Pamela hides his phone until after Christmas."

Her dad took a big bite of ham, then chewed and swallowed. "Melody seems nice."

"She is."

"Bit of a surprise, her showing up."

"No warning at all."

"You managed it well."

"Thanks."

"Just as you always do." He stopped eating to give her his full attention. She felt the weight of his gaze, his grey eyes holding hers, a serious expression on his wide face. "So tell me. How is New York treating my little girl?"

He asked this question often. To him, New York was something alive, something that roared and belched, something wild and raw and untamed, something more than a little dangerous. The idea of his only child living in its grip had always filled him with unease.

"I'm fine, Dad," she said as patiently as she could. "Work keeps me really busy. Lately I've been dealing a lot with Melody."

"How about your college friends? You see much of them?"

She shrugged. "Not as much as I'd like." As the words left her mouth, she realized it had been over a month since she'd seen any of them. Everyone was so busy with their jobs or studies. A get-together was definitely needed. She made a mental note to start organizing a weekend brunch in January.

"How about dating? Met anyone new?"

She paused before answering. Many fathers were uncomfortable discussing boys or dating with their daughters, but her dad had never hesitated about diving right in. His approach was, as always, direct and straightforward. He wasn't one of the girls, so to speak, but he wanted and expected to know the basics, which she appreciated.

"Not lately, no," she said.

"You broke off with that fellow Brad last year, right? Nothing since then? Not even one date?"

She shook her head. "I've been … busy."

He sighed. "Honey." He took another bite of ham, weighing his words, then continued. "You're young. Now is the time for you to be out there. If you're working all the time, if you're not spending time with your friends, how are you going to meet someone?"

She felt her cheeks flush. He was right, of course. For the past year, she'd been burying herself in her job. She hadn't been giving New York a chance. Again, the thought came: She was missing something…. But what?

Before she could probe deeper, her dad pushed his chair back and stood up. "How about some hot cider?"

She smiled. "You bet." Her dad's hot cider wasn't fancy — apple juice, stirred with cinnamon, heated in the microwave — but the very thought of it filled her with longing. Hot cider wasn't truly hot cider unless it was made by him.

She watched him get it ready to pop into the microwave. As she did, she remembered that her love life — or, to be precise, her lack of one — wasn't the only romantic topic ripe for discussion. She sat up straighter in her chair and said, in as innocent a tone as she could manage, "Peggy seems nice."

Her dad looked up from his stirring, nervousness flaring in his eyes. "She is." He placed the mugs in the microwave, hit the timer, then sat back down at the table. "She told me you'd figured out that she and I are … seeing each other."

"Melody picked up on it right away. Took me a bit longer."

"I was planning on telling you tonight," he said, a sheepish look on his face.

"You could have told me sooner, over the phone."

"I know, and I'm sorry." His eyes searched her face, looking for clues to how she felt. "I had it in my head that it would be better to tell you in person."

"How did the two of you meet?"

"She applied for a part-time job this spring. I saw right away how good she was, so I kept giving her more and more responsibilities, and she kept taking on more and more, so we ended up spending more and more time together…."

He looked rather awkward now — adorably self-conscious, in fact. She suppressed a smile. She could have taken pity and eased him along — soothed his anxiety with a few well-chosen words — but she held back. A few seconds of squirming seemed an appropriate punishment for him not sharing his big news sooner.

Her resolve lasted all of four seconds. He was her dad, after all — and she was such a softie!

"Dad," she said, reaching out to cover his hand with hers, "I'm happy for you. For both of you. Peggy seems great. If she makes you happy, then I'm all in, one hundred percent."

The microwave pinged. He stood up, relieved to have the distraction, and went to get the cider. The instant he opened the microwave door, the cider's wonderful aroma filled the kitchen.

"Smells so good," she said.

Grinning, he brought their mugs to the table and sat down. She took hold of her mug with both hands and let the heat seep in, then brought the mug to her nose and inhaled the lovely scent.

He said, "You sure you're okay with me dating?"

"Yes, completely okay with it." She took a sip — heavenly — then set the mug down and gave him her full attention. "I know that Mom would want you to get out there, too."

He blinked as his eyes filled with sudden tears. "Honey, I...." He stopped, coughed, and continued. "I want you to know something important. Even if things between me and Peggy go the way they seem to be going, I'll never stop loving your mom."

"I know, Dad."

He swallowed to hold back a wave of emotion. "Sometimes, you know, I talk to her. Just once in a while. I walk into the kitchen or the bedroom, and I feel like she's here."

Now it was Clara's turn to blink back tears. "I still talk with her, too. All the time."

Her dad reached out and squeezed her hand. "She's so proud of you."

"You think so?"

"Definitely. Her greatest wish was for you to be happy — to pursue your dreams, to live life to the fullest and on your own terms. And that's exactly what you've done. You've grown into such a smart, confident, beautiful young woman."

Okay, both of them were getting blubbery now. The table was about to turn into a Cane family sob-fest. "Look at the two of us," she said. "A couple of big crybabies." He coughed again but didn't argue as she brought her napkin to her eyes and dabbed her tears away. "The last thing Mom would want is for the two of us to be bawling over hot cider in the kitchen, two nights before Christmas."

He laughed, then picked up his mug and took a big swallow. "For the record, Peggy and I are taking things slow."

"I know."

"She's not looking to rush into anything, and neither am I."

"I know."

"So don't be looking for any big announcements anytime soon."

"I know."

"She's really looking forward to getting to know you."

"I know."

He grinned. "Think you know it all, do you?"

She grinned back. "Try me."

"Okay...." He thought for a moment. "Do you know that the cookie contest...."

"Wasn't your idea? Yes, I know."

"Do you know that the idea for you and Luke to partner up...."

"Wasn't your idea? That Peggy and Melody put you up to it? Yes, I know."

"Good," he said, the sheepish look coming back. "I don't usually...."

"Give much thought to cookie contests? Yes, I know."

"Well, one thing I know is that Luke Matthews has grown into a good man."

She shot him a warning look. "Yes...."

"Okay, but how about this: Unlike everyone else in this town, I'm not going to try to push you two together."

Her eyes widened in surprise. "I'm ... glad to hear that."

"Finally — something you didn't know."

She couldn't help it — she had to ask. "Out of curiosity.... Why?"

"Because you're a New York gal now," he said. "And he's a Heartsprings Valley guy."

"Ah," she said. "I see." And she did see. As was usually the case with her dad, his reasoning was no-nonsense. Direct. Straightforward.

He shrugged. "It's pretty simple. If you lived here, or if he lived there, then I might think different."

"I see."

"I'd love to have you move back home — you know that. But I also know that my little girl is all grown up now and capable of making her own decisions."

For the umpteenth time that day, tears threatened. What the heck was going on with her? Why was she so unsettled? With difficulty, she pushed down the emotional surge. "I appreciate that, Dad. Thank you."

"Just know you'll always be my little girl." He rubbed his hands together and surveyed the remains of the meal — they'd finished off every single bite. "I'll clean this up and get the plates into the dishwasher."

She glanced at the clock and was surprised to see it was after nine o'clock. The day had flown by. "Want me to help?"

He took her plate and stood up. "No, I'm good."

She followed him to the dishwasher. "I've missed this. These moments, one-on-one with my dad."

He turned around and pulled her in for another long hug. "I've missed them, too. Merry Christmas, Clara."

"Merry Christmas, Dad."

CHAPTER 25

*C*lara awoke the next morning to the sound of her phone alarm buzzing on the pillow next to her head. She reached out from under her comforter and tapped the snooze option, then quickly dropped back into delicious slumber. The snooze option offered ten lovely extra minutes of sleep, a timeframe her body understood instinctively. A minute or so before the alarm went off again, she once again became aware of her surroundings. With a sigh and a stretch, her body still cocooned in the cozy warmth of her bed, she allowed her mind to move forward in time to what would soon be happening.

A bake-off.

Against Luke Matthews.

In her kitchen.

On Christmas Eve.

Never in a million years would she have imagined this happening. She'd dreamed of a lot of Luke-related possibilities as a heartsick teenager, but competing against him in a baking contest? Not once.

Her phone buzzed again. She tapped the alarm off and, with a sigh, tugged her covers from her head and opened her eyes. She'd slept well, thank goodness, which wasn't surprising, given how crazy-busy she'd been the day before. She listened for sounds of her dad moving around the house, but didn't hear anything. That made sense — he was most likely already at the store, getting ready for another busy day.

Today would be busy for her as well. But hopefully not as insane as the day before. No rushing today, no sirree.

She picked up her phone and pressed the start button and —

Wait. What the —?

The clock said it was 9:12 a.m. How was that possible? She'd set the alarm for 8 a.m.

Or maybe she hadn't? Frantically, she checked the alarm time and saw it was set for —

9 a.m.?

Gah!

Luke was due at 10 a.m.!

She lurched upright, not even bothering to look for her slippers as she dashed into the bathroom to begin a second day of frantic preparations. In the shower, she raced through her morning routine, shampooing and soaping up in record time, marveling all the while how she had somehow screwed up her morning once again. What the heck was going on with her? Usually she was so on top of important details like this. Why was she feeling so behind the curve all of a sudden?

Gah!

A few rushed minutes later, shower completed, she found herself at a crossroads: Should she spend her precious few remaining minutes getting herself ready, or getting the kitchen ready? If her hair was going to be straightened, she wouldn't have time to get the kitchen spotless. If she focused on getting everything downstairs spic-and-span for her guest, then her naturally curly hair was going to stay naturally curly.

She sighed at her reflection in the steamed-up mirror. There really was no contest. *Hair it is*, she told herself.

Decision made, she threw herself into the task, carefully running her hair under the blow dryer and slowly straightening out the curls. Having committed herself, she didn't rush, instead focusing on doing a good job.

Finally, after what seemed like an hour but was probably closer to fifteen minutes, she finished. Which meant she had time — barely — to focus on her face. A bit of blush for her cheeks — just a hint —

to add color to her pale skin. Mascara to beef up the woefully inadequate lashes she'd been born with. A soft red lip gloss — again, just a touch — to make her lips appear a bit plumper.

She examined herself in the mirror. Was she too made-up now? It was still morning, after all. And the bake-off wasn't meant to be anything special. Just a casual get-together between two friends. She could call Luke a friend, right? Normally she wouldn't worry this much about her appearance if a friend was coming over, but so what? A good impression was important. Especially with new friends.

Yes, a new friend. That was the best way to think of him. Someone she might happen to see, maybe even hang out with from time to time, when she visited Heartsprings Valley.

Something about that train of thought stirred up her anxiety, but she firmly pushed away the impulse to dig further. *Focus*, she told herself. Her face was fine. Now, wardrobe time. She left the bathroom and padded back to her bedroom. She'd been so tired the previous night that she hadn't even bothered to unpack her small suitcase, which now lay open in the middle of the floor.

She frowned as she rifled through the clothes she'd brought. She'd worn her best sweater the day before, so that option was out, but she could wear her favorite black slacks again if she wore an apron to protect them from kitchen spills.

But what to wear instead of the sweater.... She picked up a white collared button-down shirt and held it in front of her. Not her first choice, but she hadn't planned on dressing to impress during her Heartsprings Valley trip and beggars couldn't be choosers.

Two minutes later, clothes selected and on, she slipped into her go-to black pumps (the extra two inches of height were always good for a confidence boost), then stood up to give herself a final look in the full-length mirror hanging from the closet door. She glanced at the clock: 9:58 a.m.

If Luke was a few minutes late, then she might have just enough time to get everything ready in the kitchen. She made her way downstairs, scanning the hallway for cleanup opportunities. Thankfully, her dad liked things on the neat side (a trait she'd inherited), so not much was needed beyond stacking the mail into a single pile on the sideboard in the entry hall. She moved into the kitchen and was relieved to see that things were in pretty good shape generally.

She glanced at the oven clock: 10:00 a.m. *Please be a few minutes late*, she implored Luke silently. She grabbed a clean sponge from the cabinet under the sink, dabbed a bit of dish soap on it, and gave the sink a quick scrub. After rinsing the soap away, she turned her attention to the countertop, running a damp paper towel over it.

What next? What was missing? The answer came with a jolt:

Caffeine!

Clearly, she was in desperate need of a massive infusion. Luke would probably want some, too. Plus, there was something so welcoming about the aroma of fresh-brewed coffee. Firmly in autopilot mode now, she grabbed ground coffee from the freezer — enough for four cups — and added it to the coffee maker.

She took a deep breath and hit the "Start" button.

As the familiar sounds started whirring, she slowly exhaled. Part of her still couldn't believe Luke Matthews was coming to her house. Thank goodness she'd grown up a bit and learned how to deal with surprises. Thank goodness she now possessed a modicum of poise, earned through experience.

Nevertheless, at the sound of a truck pulling up outside, her heartbeat quickened. She rinsed her hands, dried them on the hand towel hanging next to the sink, and gave the kitchen one final inspection.

Okay, she was ready. Game on, Luke Matthews.

Game on!

CHAPTER 26

*S*he heard him knock as she approached the front door. After running her tongue over her teeth and checking her face one last time in the entry hall mirror — *all clear* — she took a deep breath, squared her shoulders, and opened the door.

Crisp winter air rushed in as she gazed upon her baking opponent. He stood on the welcome mat, a friendly grin on his handsome face, a grocery bag under one arm and a cloth-covered wicker basket tucked under the other.

"Morning," Clara said, stepping aside to usher him in. "Let's get you inside."

"Thanks." He stepped in, his eyes wandering briefly over the entry hall as she shut the door behind him.

"It's a cold one this morning," she said.

"Sure is."

She gestured toward the basket and bag. "Let me help you with those."

"Thanks." He handed her the basket. She took it in both arms and found it was heavier than she expected.

"What's this?" she asked.

"A Christmas gift for you and your dad, from my mom."

"That is so thoughtful of her." Beneath the cloth cover, she caught a tantalizing whiff of fresh-baked treats. "Whatever your mom put in here smells delicious. She did *not* have to do this. Please thank her."

"I'll do that." He set the grocery bag — which appeared to be full — on the entry hall sideboard, then shrugged out of his winter coat and hung it on the rack next to her coat. He'd chosen to wear a blue button-down collared shirt this morning, a step up from his flannel shirt of the day before. It was a good color for him — the blue brought out the arctic blue of his eyes. He'd left it open at the collar, with a crisp white t-shirt peeking out from underneath. He'd shaved, she noted, and his short-cropped blond hair glowed with cleanliness.

He's dressed to impress, she thought, even as she batted the idea away. Not to impress *her*, of course — how silly to let that cross her mind. Such nonsense had no place in her brain — she was a grown woman now, not a silly teenage girl. Most likely he'd dressed up because he was being considerate of her as a new friend. Or because he had other events to attend later. Whatever the reason, it wasn't because of her. *After all, we're just baking cookies. As new friends.*

She gestured to the grocery bag. "Let me guess. The ingredients for your grandma's cookies?"

He grinned and picked up the bag from the side-board. Even though the bag appeared to be full to bursting, he handled it effortlessly. "Everything I need to win."

"Ha," she said, grinning back. "You wish. This way to the field of battle." Basket in her arms, she led him into the kitchen. "Set yourself up at the counter, anywhere you like."

He set his grocery bag on the counter next to the sink. She brought the basket to the small dining table, then fingered the cloth covering. "May I?"

"Please."

She pulled back the cloth and gasped. Inside was a mouth-watering bounty of holiday goodies. On one side were a stack of beautifully decorated ginger-bread cookies shaped like ginger men and women, all of them smiling up at her. The guys and gals were decked out in holiday hats, coats, ties, and dresses made with a delightful mix of red, green, and white icing. Next to the gingerbread folks was a hearty pile of chocolate thumbprint cookies, each with a rich dab of melted chocolate nestled in a cocoon of white shortbread. And on the right, lined up in a row, were a dozen candy canes, oh so tempting with their bright swirling colors.

"Luke," she said, unable to tear her eyes away from the lovely display, "this is so beautiful."

From his spot at the counter, where he was unloading cookie ingredients from the grocery bag, he gave her a grin. "Mom loves Christmas. Goes all out. And not just in the kitchen — also with decorating. She's a decorating madwoman."

Clara laughed. "Sounds like the two of you are close."

"She's the greatest."

"I bet she's happy you're back home in Heartsprings Valley."

"Definitely."

"And now you get to enjoy her baking all the time."

"She shows her love through her food." He patted his belly ruefully. "If I'm not careful, all that love is gonna go right here."

Her eyebrows rose as she looked at his trim waist. He had nothing to worry about when it came to his weight. Clearly, he was very fit. The job helped, no doubt, since it kept him busy and moving around. From the way his muscular shoulders pressed against his shirt, it looked like he worked out regularly, too.

She frowned as she realized what her eyes were doing. A flush of embarrassment blossomed on her cheeks. She was looking at him like she had years ago, and *that would not do*. She felt like marching herself upstairs to give herself a stern talking-to, followed by a swift kick in the you-know-what. Yes, he was attractive and fit. He'd been cute ten years ago and was just as handsome — maybe even more so — now. She simply needed to get over that. They were new friends now.

That was all!

The coffee machine chose that moment to *ping* in agreement. Grateful for the distraction and reminded again how essential it was for her to get caffeine into her system to help her poorly functioning brain work better, she covered the basket of treats back up and said, "I've made coffee. You want some?"

"That'd be great."

She slipped past him to the coffee pot, which was now ready to enjoy. From an upper cabinet, she got out two big mugs. One was her favorite — a curvy deep-red mug she'd made with her mom in a summer pottery class when she was twelve. The other was a memento from a high school fund-raiser — a beefy white mug with the Heartsprings Valley High Panthers logo on it.

She poured coffee into the mugs, then turned to her guest. "Black, a dash of sugar?"

"You remembered," he said with a grin.

"Of course." She added half a spoonful of sugar to the Panthers mug, stirred, and set it in front of him.

She turned to the fridge, got out a small carton of cream, and splashed a healthy dollop into hers.

With a sigh of relief, she brought the mug to her nose and inhaled the life-enhancing aroma.

Luke, who was watching her closely, grinned. "You sure do like your coffee, don't you?"

"You remembered," she replied, her eyes holding his.

"Of course." He raised his mug. "To our upcoming battle. May the best cookie win."

"May the best cookie win," she agreed as she clinked her mug on his.

CHAPTER 27

*S*he took a sip. As caffeinated goodness rolled over her taste buds, she felt herself returning to a more normal state of mind. She inhaled deeply, luxuriating in the coffee's heat. Sometimes, in rare idle moments, she dreamed of spending every moment of every day in a coffee shop, watching the world pass by from her favorite chair at her favorite table near a big sunny window. Always with a fresh hot mug warming her hands, the steam from the brew enveloping her in its heavenly aroma.

"So," she heard him say, drawing her out of her reverie. "How should we do this bake-off?"

He was asking about her plan. That was good. Plans were good. Useful for all kinds of things, including distracting herself from unwanted musings.

"The plan," she said to buy time, since her over-sleeping fiasco meant she had not yet had time to formulate one, "is to have our cookies ready for our judges when they arrive."

"What time will that be?"

Good question. "Noonish, I think. I'll text Melody and Barbara to confirm."

"How much should we share about our recipes?"

Another interesting question. She was curious about his grandmother's recipe, and certainly it would be easy enough to look to see how different it was from hers. But maybe there was a better way — a way that would be more fun?

"How about we share nothing and keep every-thing mysterious until after the bake-off is over?"

He chuckled. "Build the suspense? I like it. One thing I will share: Grandma's recipe requires the dough to chill before I roll it out."

"Same with my mom's recipe."

"So...." He glanced at the oven's clock. "We should probably get started now."

"Let's get you set up." She set her coffee on the counter, opened a lower cabinet, and pulled out a set of mixing bowls. "I assume you'll need a bowl for dry and a bowl for mixing?"

He pulled a recipe card out of his pocket and consulted it. "That's right. My mom said it's impor-tant for the butter and sugar to cream really well so the dough is light and fluffy."

He'd discussed the recipe with his mom — another interesting fact. Maybe he wasn't as confident about his kitchen skills as he seemed?

"Very important," she agreed. "We can take turns with the mixer." From a different lower cabinet, she grabbed her mom's mixer and set it on the counter. It wasn't a new model — her mom had bought it more than a decade ago — but it had been start-of-the-art back then and still had lots of good mixing left in it. In the morning light, its brushed-nickel finish looked reassuringly solid.

She glanced at his ingredients on the counter. "You brought everything you need?"

"Yep."

"Okay, I'll get my ingredients." She opened the freezer and pulled out flour and confectioners' sugar, then opened the fridge for the butter and eggs. From the pantry, she gathered the vanilla extract, baking powder, kosher salt, and cream of tartar. Then, from the utensils drawer, she grabbed spatulas and measuring cups and spoons.

"I see you don't need a recipe to know what you need," he said.

She shrugged. "My mom and I used to make sugar cookies every Christmas."

"Sounds like I'm in trouble."

"Big trouble."

He grinned and grabbed a bowl. "According to my grandma's amazing recipe, which I have promised to execute faithfully to the best of my ability to guarantee a win for the Matthews family, I start by whisking together the dry ingredients."

She liked his easy confidence, and the way he wielded his sense of humor. She reached into the implements drawer and got out measuring cups and spoons. "You'll need these."

He picked up the measuring cup, dipped the cup into his flour, and shook it gently to remove excess flour. But he wasn't done: He brought the cup to eye level, then picked up a measuring spoon and ran the flat edge over the lip of the cup to remove even more flour. "Here goes." He added the flour to the bowl, then dipped the cup into the flour bag for a second helping.

She got busy with her own dry ingredients. With a practiced eye, she tossed flour, baking powder, and salt into her dry bowl and whisked them up.

Because he was being more careful, Luke took longer to finish. In a way, he was being smart: Baking rewarded precision. But no amount of careful measuring was going to change the simple fact that her victory in the bake-off was already assured, thanks to her buttery advantage.

He grabbed the whisk and gave his dry ingredients a thorough mixing, a look of concentration on his face. She'd noticed the same focus yesterday, while they were wrapping gifts for the window display. He had the ability to really zoom in on something and give it his undivided attention.

He looked up when he was done. "Okay," he said, somewhat self-consciously, perhaps realizing that she'd been watching him.

"Time for butter and sugar," she said. "How about you go first?"

"No," he said, "I'll follow your lead."

He watched her add butter and confectioners' sugar to the bowl. She set the bowl in the mixer and turned it on. The sturdy mixer got to churning, quickly combining the butter and sugar.

"It takes a couple of minutes to get the right consistency," she said. "While we're waiting, I want to hear about the Army. We were about to talk about it yesterday when we got interrupted."

"Sure," he said. "Happy to tell you all about it."

"Start with the basics. Where did you serve, and what did you do?"

He took a sip from his coffee, his eyes on hers. "I joined after high school — I think you know that." When she nodded, he continued. "I've always been good with mechanicals and woodworking, and I knew from helping my dad during summer breaks that I liked fixing stuff, so I told the recruiter that I wanted to be part of a team that worked construction."

"You mean, like building Army barracks and runways and things like that?"

"Exactly."

The sugar-butter mix was starting to look nice and fluffy. She turned off the mixer, grabbed a spatula, and scraped down the walls of the bowl.

"So," she said as she put the bowl back in the mixer and picked up an egg, "it sounds like you got to do what you hoped to do?"

"I did. Our unit moved around a lot, and we worked on a lot of very different projects."

She cracked an egg in the bowl and turned the mixer on. "Where did they send you?"

"Back and forth between stateside and Kuwait twice. Also short deployments to Diego Garcia — that's an island in the Indian Ocean — and Afghanistan."

"Afghanistan?" she said as she cracked another egg into the mixer. "Was that dangerous?"

He nodded. "It was. But our unit got in and out without a problem."

"I'm glad to hear that."

He took a deep breath, then exhaled. "I get asked this question a lot, so let me go ahead and answer: No, I never saw combat."

She'd been wondering exactly that. "Not even once?"

He shook his head. "Combat is a real and present danger in places like Afghanistan. But most of us don't serve in places like that, and most of us never fire a hostile shot."

She realized her chest was tight with tension at the thought of him being in harm's way. "I'm glad," she said as she added a second egg.

He gave her a wry grin. "The much bigger risk was the heat."

Her eyebrows rose. "You mean, in Kuwait?"

"Hottest place I've ever been," he said with grim shake of his head. "Couldn't wait to get out."

"And head back home to the crisp wintry air of Heartsprings Valley?"

"You have no idea."

"I might. New York in the summer gets pretty bad, too."

"One hundred thirty degrees bad?"

She gasped. "One hundred *thirty* degrees? Okay, you win."

He laughed. "My first victory of the day."

"And your last," she shot right back, softening the volley with a grin. She had one last ingredient to add: vanilla. She tossed in a good dash — again without measuring — and watched it blend into the fluffy dough.

With a start, she realized that Luke was looking at her with admiration. "I'm up against a real expert, aren't I?"

She held his gaze. "Scared?"

His gaze intensified. "Terrified. Quaking in my boots."

With a pleased glow, she returned her attention to

the mixer. She dropped the speed to low, picked up the bowl of dry ingredients, and added them to the dough.

"Won't be long now," she said. Together, they watched the dry mix get blended in.

"How long?" he asked as he inched closer for a better look.

"Only as long as needed."

"A minute? Two minutes?"

"Something like that." She noted the hint of concern in his tone. Like most new bakers, he wanted to avoid mistakes by measuring and timing everything.

After examining the dough for several seconds, she nodded and turned off the mixer. "Done." She reached down and grabbed a prep board from a lower cabinet drawer, then opened another drawer for plastic wrap. She set both on the counter next to the prep space she'd been using. "After I scrape out my dough, this is all yours."

"Thanks."

"You know what to do?"

He hesitated, just for a second. "I think so. I'll ask if I need help."

"Sounds good."

She had just finished scraping her dough onto the plastic wrap on the wooden prep board when her phone buzzed in her pocket. She handed him the bowl, then pulled her phone out of her pocket and sighed softly when she saw who it was:

Melody.

CHAPTER 28

$\mathcal{L}$uke heard the sigh. "Trouble?"

"I hope not." She brought the phone to her ear. "Good morning, Melody. How are you?"

"I'm wonderful, darling," her client replied, her voice rich and full of enthusiasm. "Just wonderful. This town is such a treasure." In the background, she heard another woman — Barbara, no doubt — saying something that caused Melody to laugh.

"Say hi to Barbara," Clara said.

"Darling, she insisted I call to ask how you and Luke are making out with the bake-off."

"We're just getting started," Clara replied evenly, choosing to ignore the irrepressible nosiness of just about every single person in this town. "So far, so good."

"Barbara and Stu have agreed to help judge. We're so excited!"

Strangely enough, her client sounded sincere — like she actually was excited about a cookie bake-off, in an ordinary house, in an ordinary kitchen, in a town she barely knew, with no cameras flashing and no audience watching her every move. What in the world had come over her famous client, the media-savvy, award-winning Broadway singer-dancer-actress with the Hollywood boyfriend and the glamorous jet-setting life, who routinely asked for elephants and nearly always got them?

"I'm ... glad to hear that," Clara said. "You sure everything's okay over there?"

"Darling, more than okay. Barbara just made the most amazing croissants, which we now are slathering with the most delicious butter. I'm in heaven!"

That brought a smile to her lips. Barbara's croissants were legendary. And the butter — well, there was no mystery there. "Glad you're in good hands."

"The best. Now, what time do you want us there?"

"Noonish okay?"

"Noonish it is. Ta *ta* for now!"

Melody clicked off, Clara sighed, and Luke looked over from his spot in front of the mixer, where he was adding butter and confectioners' sugar to the bowl.

"Do we need to start looking for an elephant?"

She laughed. "No. Which is a bit odd. She's usually so … grand in her thinking. Normally right about now I'd be tearing out my hair, trying to figure out how to deliver the impossible."

"What's she up to?" He set his bowl into the mixer, set it to low, and turned it on. Gently but thoroughly, the mixer got to work churning his ingredients.

"She and Barbara are just gabbing away in the kitchen, baking croissants. They'll be over around noon to judge our cookies."

He shrugged. "I'm glad she's enjoying herself. Nice to have a change of pace, especially when everything's going nonstop."

How true. For her client, at least, Heartsprings Valley was offering exactly that: a break, a respite, from the high-pressure life of a Broadway star.

But what about her client's publicity assistant, the overworked Clara Cane? So far, she'd had nothing even approaching a break. She'd been as busy here as she was in New York.

But perhaps it was wrong for her to think like that. Perhaps it was wrong to expect life to move at a slower pace in a small town. Certainly Luke had been busy since his return home — managing the family contracting business with his dad, running from job to job to job, and now here in her kitchen…. She watched him lean over the bowl, examining the sugar and butter as it churned. Just as she'd done a few minutes before, he nodded to himself when it reached the right consistency, turned off the mixer, picked up a spatula, scraped the edges of the bowl, returned the bowl to the mixer, cracked an egg into the bowl, and turned the mixer back on. He didn't have her natural flair — the kitchen was obviously not his territory — but it was clear he'd watched her and learned. He probably approached all of life's challenges the same way: observing closely, learning what he needed to do, then adapting and delivering.

"How am I doing?" he asked.

"Great," she replied frankly. And he was, just as he excelled at so many other things — applying the same skill set he'd had all the way back in high school, when he led his high school team to the state football championship.

"So..." she said as she watched him add a second egg to the bowl, "getting back to the Army. What was the biggest project you worked on?"

"The biggest?" he said without looking up from the bowl. "A partnership with the Kuwaiti government for a new hospital. Unlike a lot of the temporary structures we built, the hospital was designed to be permanent. Took us eighteen months."

"I imagine there are a lot of differences between temporary and permanent buildings."

"Tons." He added vanilla, then picked up the bowl of dry ingredients and began mixing them in. "Temporary structures need to be strong, but the materials aren't selected for durability. The focus is on speed of construction and flexibility of design."

"But a permanent hospital?"

"Totally different story. We built it to last fifty years, even longer. In a climate as harsh as that one, that's a challenge. Plus, as a medical facility, we had to factor in who the building is for."

"Patients versus soldiers?"

"Exactly. Especially with the pediatric wing for the kids."

"Oh," she said, surprised.

He looked up from the bowl. "You weren't expecting that."

She nodded. "I guess not. When I think of the Army...."

"You don't think of hospitals for sick kids."

"Right."

He shrugged. "Every once in a while, that's what we do. It was a good project. I'm glad I was part of it."

"Were you there when it opened?"

He turned off the mixer. His dough was ready. He took the bowl out of the mixer and picked up the spatula. Without being asked, she pulled out the plastic wrap and placed it over a cutting board next to hers.

"We were finishing up the electrical in the other wing when the pediatric wing opened, so they brought us over to meet the doctors and nurses and patients." He paused to scrape his dough onto the plastic wrap. "Seeing the kids there really drove home how important our work was."

"You got to meet the kids?"

He smiled. "They were great. Curious, grateful, and brave."

Tears began to well up, but she blinked them away. "I'm glad you had the chance to do that."

"Me, too. A lot of kids were really sick, but the way they handled themselves...." For a second it seemed like he was getting emotional, too — his eyes seemed brighter than before — but he recovered and squared his shoulders. "Like I said, glad I was able to help."

He clapped his hands together and turned toward her. "So, Ms. Cane. What next?"

CHAPTER 29

*C*lara blinked under the force of his gaze, temporarily frozen in place. Part of her deer-in-the-headlights response was due to his distracting physical presence, of course. She already knew she was susceptible — clearly she needed to up her defenses. But there was more going on than just that. She'd felt the tug of an emotional connection. His affection for the kids had touched her heart.

The room was becoming warmer. Her breath quickened.

"Nothing," she finally said. "I mean, we need to cool this dough down." *And not just the dough.* "It's too hot in here right now."

"Right," he said, his blue eyes not shying away. "Too hot. That's not good."

"Not good at all." She took a deep breath and willed herself to calm down. "Okay." Another deep breath, then: "Let's break our dough in half, then flatten it into disks about an inch thick. Then we'll wrap the disks and put them in the fridge to chill."

"Got it." He ripped his gaze from her — regretfully, it seemed — then separated his dough and began flattening it out.

She turned to her dough and did the same, tension easing away as she focused on her task. Quickly, standing side by side, they flattened and wrapped in silence, as if grateful to have something straightforward to focus on.

He finished a few seconds before her. "Ready when you are."

She wrapped the dough disks, picked them up, opened the fridge, and set them on the lowest shelf, his disks on the right and hers on the left. "We'll put them down here. The fridge is colder on the bottom shelf."

"Got it."

She closed the door and stood up. "And now...."

"We chill while the dough chills?"

"We chill while the dough chills." As the words tumbled out of her mouth, she realized she had no plan for this period of waiting. A glance at the wall clock — it was just past 10:30 a.m. — told her that she had at least *ninety minutes* of quality alone time with Luke. Desperately, she tried to push away the wave of anxiety that threatened to rush over her. What in the world were the two of them going to do for ninety minutes?

"I have an idea for what to do next," he said, as if reading her mind.

"Great," she said, perhaps too gratefully. "What's that?"

He nodded toward the grocery bag he'd brought with him. "I have the ingredients for my mom's hot cocoa. How about we make some?"

She exhaled with relief. She loved hot cocoa — *adored* it. "That sounds perfect."

"Good. It's an essential Christmas tradition in the Matthews household."

"A fantastic tradition it is. I wholeheartedly approve."

He grinned as he took the ingredients out of the bag. As expected, she saw milk, cocoa powder, vanilla extract, sugar, salt, and cinnamon.

"Looks like we're covered," she said. "Anything I can add?"

"Do you have a bowl and a whisk we can stick in the freezer so they're cold enough for the whipped cream?"

Whipped cream — yum. "Absolutely." She grabbed a whisk from the utensils drawer. "Do you want to use the mixer, or whisk by hand?"

"I usually do it by hand, so let's stick with that."

"Got it." She opened a lower cabinet and picked out a stainless steel mixing bowl, then set the bowl and whisk in the freezer. "These should chill nicely by the time we need them."

"Great," he said. He stared at his ingredients lined up on the counter as he focused on his plan of attack.

"Saucepan?" she asked.

"Yes, please."

She reached down and placed a saucepan in front of him. "What else?"

"Stirring spoon."

She grabbed one and set it down. "What else?"

He turned and gave her a smile. "Someone really wants hot cocoa."

"You have no idea."

He laughed. "I think we have what we need."

"Anything I can help with?"

"Can you be the designated stirrer?"

"Done."

"Then let's get started."

He poured milk into the saucepan — enough for four cups, she noted with pleasure — set the pan on a burner, turned the burner to medium-low, and watched the flame whoosh to life. He adjusted the flame down just a bit and nodded, satisfied. "Too much heat too fast isn't good. I learned that lesson the hard way."

She nodded. "A slow buildup is always better."

Carefully, he measured the sugar while they waited for the first tell-tale wisps of steam to rise from the warming milk. Once again, she noticed how attentive he was to detail and how good he was at focusing in on whatever it was he was doing. Once he aimed for something, he went after it with dedication and energy. She had a similar capacity for concentration, at least in spurts, but she also knew how easily she could be pulled out of her zone by competing events. Perhaps, if she thought about it a different way, her approach was just more flexible, intuitive, and responsive.

Which way was better? Perhaps their cookies would soon give them a hint.

"Time for sugar," he said, interrupting her train of thought and pulling her back to the here and now.

She picked up the spoon. "Ready to stir," she said.

He measured out the sugar and sprinkled it into the heated milk, then followed with the cocoa. "It won't take long to melt in."

Indeed, almost like magic, the cocoa and sugar dissolved effortlessly. As he reached over the pan to add the remaining ingredients, his arm brushed her shoulder and she caught a hint of his aftershave. The sudden awareness of his closeness brought a flush to her cheeks — a flush that only deepened as she chastised herself for not responding in a more grown-up, level-headed manner.

Compounding everything, he glanced at her face and noticed her pink cheeks. *Gah!*

"It's getting steamy in here," he said.

"Mmm," she said, noting he wasn't budging from

his spot. She became extremely aware that if she wasn't careful, her shoulder would brush his arm again. "The cocoa's looking good," she said, desperately hoping to refocus her attention on something safer. "And it smells great, too."

She risked another glance up and saw him looking right back at her. His gaze didn't waver. "I agree," he said, his voice low and soft, the blue of his eyes drawing her in like a magnet. "Looking really good."

Gah! She inhaled sharply and took a step back, her heart and mind racing. What was she thinking? What was wrong with her? Why was she reading more into this situation than was really there? "I can't wait for the whipped cream," she said as brightly as she could manage. "The bowl and whisk should be nicely chilled by now."

He didn't move for a long second, his eyes still on her. Then a small smile appeared on his lips and his shoulders relaxed. "Of course," he said. "Time for whipped cream." He eased past her, opened the freezer, took out the bowl and whisk, poured the heavy cream into the bowl, and got to work on the whisking, really putting muscle into the effort. Before long, the cream was almost ready to peak. He grabbed the confectioners' sugar and, without measuring, dashed in a good helping, followed by a similar dash of vanilla extract.

From the smoothness and fluency of his movements, it was clear he'd whipped a lot of cream.

"You're good at this," she said.

He shrugged as he brought the peaks closer and closer to perfection. "Let's just say I had incentive growing up. The more cream I whisked, the more cocoa I got."

She grinned. "Okay if we use the same mugs we used for coffee?"

"Yep." He glanced at the cocoa on the stove, which was now simmering beautifully. "Pour when you're ready."

"Oh, I'm so ready." She took her red mug and his white mug, rinsed them in the sink, then set them on the counter next to the stove. She turned the burner to the lowest setting, picked up the saucepan, and poured cocoa into both mugs. The wonderful aroma rushed over her as the heated goodness filled the two mugs.

She set the saucepan back on the burner, then glanced at the whipped cream and gasped at the tempting peaks rising firmly from the bowl. "Oh my, that looks so delicious," she said.

He shot her a grin and picked up a spoon. "Here goes," he said.

She watched him spoon heaping dollops of whipped cream onto each mug. She leaned in and inhaled the wonderful aroma, her mouth tingling with anticipation.

"Final step," he said. She looked up and saw him with two peppermint candy canes, each about four inches high. "You want a hint of peppermint in your cocoa?"

"I'd love that."

He set a candy cane into each mug. The peppermint sank into the whipped cream until only the curved tops were visible.

He picked up her curvy red mug and handed it to her, then picked up his.

"To spending Christmas with family and friends," he said.

She clinked her mug against his. "Amen to that."

CHAPTER 30

*S*he watched him take his first sip, his eyes closing with pleasure. She followed his lead, the whipped cream and hot cocoa thrilling her taste buds and sending her, just for a second, back in time, to another Christmas long ago. She was a child again, perhaps six or seven, standing in this very spot, watching her mom pour her a different cup of cocoa. "It's hot, so be careful," her mom said as she placed the mug in Clara's tiny hands. "It's best if you drink it slowly."

"Something wrong with the cocoa?" Luke asked.

She blinked, startled. Had something in her expression changed? "Not at all," she rushed to assure him. "It's delicious. It brought back memories, that's all. Of my mom."

"Ah."

"Good memories," she emphasized. "I used to find

it painful to think too much about my mom. My memories reminded me of what I lost. But now...."

He waited silently for her to continue, his eyes not leaving her face.

"Now, they remind me of everything I was lucky enough to have. I'm so grateful to have the memories I have."

He nodded in understanding. "It takes time, doesn't it?"

"It does." She coughed to clear her throat, then took another sip of cocoa, allowing the cool cream and hot chocolate to swirl over her tongue, the hint of peppermint adding a lovely, fresh accent. "How about we head into the living room?"

"After you."

She led the way from the kitchen and gestured to the couch. "Make yourself comfortable." She set her mug on the coffee table in front of the couch and turned to the fireplace. "It's a bit chilly, so let me get the fire started."

"Need any help?"

"No, it's gas. I got this." She pressed a button on the mantel and watched the fire whoosh to life. "Dad put the unit in a few years ago. It used to be such a chore to make a fire — bringing in wood, stacking it by the fire, kneeling down to arrange the logs in the fire, then sticking newspapers between them so that the fire would get started...."

"And now?"

She shrugged. "Easy-peasy." He was still standing — very polite of him — so she gestured again to the couch. "Have a seat."

They both sat down and settled in, him on one side of the couch and her on the other. The fireplace's faux logs looked just like the real thing. Already, they were glowing red. Heat from the flames warmed her cheeks.

"The fire feels good," he said, looking around the room with interest. He pointed to a photo on the mantel of Clara and her dad and her mom, and for just a second, her stomach clenched. She had been fourteen when the photo was taken, at her gawkiest and most self-conscious — her hair cropped too short, her eyes hidden behind oversize glasses, her mouth full of metal. Normally, a photo like that would be banished to the back pages of a family photo book. But that particular photo would never be banished, because it was special and always would be. It showed her mom, active and vibrant, a few months before her health began to decline. She was in the center of the photo, with Clara on one side and her dad on the other. Arms linked, the three of them were grinning goofily at the camera, their enjoyment of the moment clear on their faces. In the background was Heartsprings Lake, the afternoon sunlight reflecting off the water. They'd been on a hike on the trail overlooking the lake, enjoying the crisp autumn air and the scent of falling leaves, when they ran into friends and her mom had impulsively whipped out her small camera and had the three of them pose for a photo.

Maybe the photo hadn't been impulsive, Clara realized. Maybe her mom, aware of what was coming, had brought the camera with her because she wanted to leave her daughter and husband with an image — a memory — of the three of them on a happy day.

"I was fourteen," she said quietly.

His sympathetic glance spoke volumes. "Looks like that was a good day. A good memory."

"Definitely." She felt tears starting, so she blinked and coughed to push them back down.

"You know," he said, deftly shifting topics, "there's still a lot you haven't told me about life in the big city."

"Oh," she said, grateful for the change of subject. "New York's great."

"You must have a lot of friends there from college."

"I do."

"Tell me about them."

She smiled at the thought of her college pals and launched eagerly into descriptions of serious Shelly and carefree Callie and headstrong Helena. Soon enough, thanks to his questions, she was telling him how they met (in their freshman dorm), how they'd bonded (too many late-night study sessions in the campus cafeteria), and what they were all doing now that college was over.

"It's great that you have a crew to do stuff with," he said.

"Yes, it's great." She sighed. "When I see them."

He raised an eyebrow. "What do you mean?"

She shifted on the couch to face him. "We're all really busy."

"With work?"

"And studies. And even though we're all in the same city, we live in different neighborhoods. It can take an hour sometimes to get from place to place."

"That's rough. I guess I expected you'd have an amazing, super-busy social life."

She snorted. "I wish."

He took a sip of his cocoa. "So you keep busy with…?"

"Work."

"Chasing elephants."

"Day and night."

"Do you miss it? A social life? Having friends and family nearby?"

She thought for a moment. "I do miss it. Even though I live in a huge city and am surrounded by millions of people and barely have time to sleep let alone enjoy myself, sometimes I feel pretty lonely."

Why had she admitted that? Was it because his eyes were so blue and expressive and gazing at her with such interest and understanding?

"Most people are afraid to admit that," he said.

"Normally, I'm one of those people."

He cocked his head. "But now?"

She fortified herself with a good sip of cocoa — half of it was gone — while she considered her answer. "I suppose I feel comfortable telling you. I trust you're not going to judge me."

He smiled. "This is a judgment-free zone." He took another sip of his cocoa. "So tell me ... what does your boyfriend think about your crazy working hours?"

CHAPTER 31

*S*omehow, she managed to avoid choking on her hot cocoa as his question penetrated her brain. For a single long second that seemed to stretch into infinity, she double-checked and then triple-checked to make sure she'd heard right:

Had *Luke Matthews* just asked *Clara Cane* about Clara Cane's *boyfriend*?

Yes, he'd done just that. But why? Why had he asked? Perhaps he was only being friendly? Making conversation? Perhaps because this was what new friends did — asked questions like that?

He's interested in you, a traitorous voice chimed in.

Such utter nonsense, she immediately countered. Only a silly teenage girl would think that. A grown woman — like the woman she was now — would know better than to leap to such an erroneous and absurd conclusion. Especially when the conclusion was so unfair — unfair to herself, and unfair to Luke. He was being friendly, that's all. Like the new friend he was.

Gah!

"Boyfriend?" she repeated, trying to buy time.

He blinked and a spot of color appeared on his cheeks. "I mean, I guess I assumed...." His voice trailed off, his discomfort clear.

She needed more time to figure out what to say. "You guess you assumed … what?"

His flush deepened. "That someone like you would have a boyfriend."

Someone like *me?* What did *that* mean? Now she needed even more time. "What do you mean, someone like me?"

He swallowed and shifted his position on the couch. "I mean," he stammered, "someone beautiful and smart like you."

The instant the words left his mouth, it was like a switch flipped inside him. Any discomfort he might have been feeling seemed to vanish. His back straightened. The blue in his eyes intensified. It was like he returned to solid ground as soon as he spoke his truth.

If so, then.... Now it was her turn to flush. The teenager still inside her started doing excited somersaults. Luke Matthews was telling her she was beautiful and smart?

"No boyfriend," she said, frightening herself with

how honestly she answered. Why had she said that? Should she have gone with a vague answer? Something along the lines of "No one at the moment," to make him think she was, in fact, dating every now and then?

Did she see relief and excitement flash through his eyes, or was she dreaming?

"I guess because you're probably too busy?" he asked.

"Oh, totally," she said, pleased he'd lobbed up a perfectly reasonable explanation. "Work is nonstop — it's been that way for months."

He picked up his cocoa from the coffee table and took a sip.

She found herself eager to fill the silence. "I was dating someone last year. Brad."

"What happened?"

"I ended it." When his eyebrows rose, she continued. "He's a great guy, someone I met in school, but we were both really busy and didn't see each other as often as either of us would have liked." She shrugged, feeling herself calming. "And when we did see each other, it didn't feel … special? It's not that anything was wrong or bad, but the spark wasn't there. It's like we were doing what we were supposed to be doing, not what we wanted to be doing."

He nodded. "It's good you were able to figure that out."

Hmm…. An interesting comment. "I hadn't thought about it that way before."

"Figuring out stuff like that is hard. It can take a long time."

"Do I sense a story?"

He paused, his eyes not leaving her face, then said, "I was engaged."

Her heart thumped. "Engaged?"

"Her name's Rosalinda. Rosie. We were in the same unit." He pulled out his phone and scrolled through photos. "Let me show you the unit." He pressed a photo and brought up a picture of eight soldiers in khakis and green tee shirts, caked with dust and dried sweat, standing in harsh sunlight in front of what looked like a temporary barracks. Luke was in the middle, grinning at the camera. Next to him was a woman, slim and attractive, with a hint of dark hair beneath her cap.

"This picture is from … Kuwait?"

He nodded. "It was incredibly hot that day. So dry and dusty it hurt to breathe."

"And this is your unit?"

"Some of us."

"The woman next to you … that's Rosie?"

"That's right."

"How long were you engaged?"

"About six months."

He seemed willing — even ready — to share, so she didn't hold back. "What happened?"

He took a deep breath and exhaled. "It's hard to explain, especially if you haven't served, but I can try." When she nodded, he continued. "When you're a soldier, your unit becomes family. A bond develops. It's about trust, about knowing you have each other's backs, about knowing you'll be there for each other no matter what. Our unit was always getting sent someplace new, to build or repair something new, often with no one else around for miles. A lot of time, it was just us."

"So you got close."

"Beyond close. These guys are my brothers. And so is Rosie."

Her brow furrowed.

"This is the part that's hard for me to explain," he said. "It took me a while to understand it enough myself."

"You're doing great so far."

"We met when she joined the unit on our second tour in Kuwait — she was training to be an engineer and was brought in to work on the hospital project. We hit it off and one thing led to another and…."

"You became a couple."

He nodded. "For a while, I thought she was the one."

"What was it about her?"

"Well, that's easy. I like smart. I like beautiful, too, but smart does it for me every time."

Clara ignored the heat that rose on her cheeks.

"And I loved how relentless she was. Especially when it came to her work. She took a lot of guff as a woman, but she didn't let that stop her."

"She sounds really great."

"She is really great."

"Is she still in the Army?"

He nodded.

"And is that why the relationship and engagement ended?"

"Sort of."

She waited for him to continue, but he seemed to be having trouble wrapping words around his thoughts, so she prompted him with a question. "You … didn't want a long-distance relationship?"

"No, it wasn't that." He took a deep breath, clearly trying to figure out which words to use. "I saw the Army as an opportunity. For me, the Army was about developing my skills and gaining experience and meeting great people and helping, at least in some small way, to make the world a better place. Basically, I saw it as a great job. I always knew I'd be coming back to Heartsprings Valley."

"What did Rosie see the Army as?"

"A career. A life."

"That's a very different outlook."

"She's from a tough background — no dad in the picture, her mom the bread-winner. Every single thing she's accomplished, she's worked incredibly hard to get. She has no interest in looking back. She wants to keep moving forward. She loves the Army. She's made it her home. "

"But for you…."

"Home has always been here." He sighed. "Neither of us understood that when we got engaged. We worked as a couple because we were both serving. Take away that structure and way of life and…."

"You realized you had very different life goals."

"In the end, too different."

They were silent for a moment, but this time the silence didn't make her nervous. It felt comfortable and natural.

"Who realized it first?" she asked.

"She did. But I wasn't far behind. We were arguing a lot. Resentments were building up. I didn't want to stay, she didn't want to leave. One afternoon, she sat me down and just let it all out — laid everything on the table, everything she was seeing and feeling and thinking and worrying about. And I realized I pretty much agreed with everything she said."

"That must have been a tough conversation."

His eyes teared up. "One of the hardest of my life. But also, in a way I never could have imagined, one of the best."

"How so?"

"I learned how important it is to communicate. Especially about what matters most."

"I'm sorry it didn't work out."

"Well…." He considered her words as he took

another sip of cocoa. "I'm actually not sorry. Don't get me wrong — it was hard at first. Every day, seeing her and working with her and hearing her voice but us not being together — that was hard. But it got easier with time. When I discharged, when I said goodbye, we left as friends."

"Have you seen her since you left?"

He shook his head. "We email. Not as often lately. She met a new guy a few months ago. A good guy, from what I hear."

"How does that sit with you?"

He shrugged, his eyes not leaving her face. "I'm happy for her. And if I'm being honest, a little sad at the same time — you can't help but wonder how things might have gone differently."

She watched his face and mouth and eyes and the set of his shoulders as he said that, looking for the subtle signs that he was being truthful with her and himself. Her gut told her that he was — that he'd figured out how to move on.

"Cute, smart, and emotionally mature — do you have no faults?"

When he blinked with surprise, she realized with a jolt that she hadn't *thought* those words — she'd *spoken* them! "Did I just say that out loud?" she gasped, her face flushing deep red.

He chuckled. "You sure did." And he chuckled some more.

"Luke, I'm so sorry."

"For what?" he said with a grin. "And for the record, I have tons of flaws. Huge flaws."

"Oh, is that so?" she said, desperate for a lifeline.

"I love big loud action movies, especially when they're really cheesy and bad."

She laughed, relief flooding through her. "Oh, that's awful."

He leaned closer. "I leave the toilet seat up sometimes."

"A truly terrible, terrible flaw."

He nodded. "Total deal-breaker, according to my mom. Who I still live with, by the way. Another flaw."

She couldn't wipe the grin off her face. "Don't tell me you live in the basement."

"Okay, I won't tell you."

"But yes?"

"You told me not to tell you."

"Oh, come on."

"I take what you say very seriously. Your wish is my command."

"I bet there's a good reason you live at home."

"Several. It's a big rambling place, so there's plenty of room. Mom and Dad like having me there. But the real reason is, I'm saving up for a house of my own."

"A future homeowner. Any sense of when?"

His gaze intensified. "Just waiting to meet the right person to help me pick the right place."

Her lungs stopped working. It felt like she had to mentally force herself to start breathing again. Which was so *annoying*. Why was her poise choosing this moment to desert her? What in the world had happened to her ability to calmly confront the unexpected?

Time to take charge of the conversation. She gestured to his phone. "Your unit. Tell me more."

He nodded, happy to oblige. Soon enough, she found herself caught up in his stories about his main buds — Mookie and Joe and Luther and Enrique and of course Rosie — and their Army misadventures. So caught up, in fact, that she almost missed the knock on the front door.

Luke paused. He'd heard the knock, too. "Our judges?"

My, how the time had flown. She sighed. "You have to promise you'll tell me later how Mookie got the tank back before they noticed it missing."

He grinned. "Promise."

She stood up. "Ready to lose, mister?"

He stood up with her. "I'm ready to *win*."

CHAPTER 32

*C*lara opened the front door and found three grinning faces on her doorstep — Melody, Barbara, and Stu — all of them looking expectant and cheerful. "Welcome," she said. "Come on in!"

They bustled in after exchanging quick hugs and greetings, all of them eager to get out of the cold.

In the entry hall, Melody unwrapped her scarf and shrugged out of her winter coat, her eyes wandering over the decor. "So this is your family home."

"Home sweet home," Clara said, shutting the door tight. "So glad you're all here."

While Luke was helping them hang up their coats, Clara noticed a grocery bag on the entry hall sideboard. "What's that?"

Stu turned and flashed her a grin. "Something to nibble on." He was a short, round man with a wide grin and a nearly bald head — a shorter, plumper version of her dad — dressed today in blue jeans and a blue sweater. "We figured you kids must have worked up an appetite with all that baking."

"You did *not* have to do that."

"Oh, yes we did," Barbara chimed in. "Have you eaten anything this morning?"

Clara turned toward her. "Sure."

"Really? What?"

"Well…. Coffee and hot cocoa."

"See?" Barbara said to Stu. "Like I said."

Stu kept his eyes on Clara. "She says New York is wearing you down. Says we need to get a bit of meat on your bones."

"A liquid diet never did anybody any good," Barbara added.

"Except as a cleanse," Melody murmured.

Barbara shot her a startled look. "A cleanse?"

"Very freeing," Melody murmured.

Barbara blinked, momentarily at a loss for words, trying to wrap her head around the strange dieting practices of the denizens of the big city. "I'll have to take your word on that, Melody."

"Guys, really, I'm fine," Clara protested.

"And hungry, I hope," Stu said. "We brought fresh biscuits and gravy."

At the mention of biscuits, Clara's stomach rumbled. "You know I can't resist those."

"Good," Stu said, then turned to Barbara. "See? Easy as pie."

"Did someone say pie?" Luke asked.

"No, but we brought fresh biscuits and gravy."

Luke grinned and picked up the bag. "You don't have to sell me — I'm in."

Together, they marched into the kitchen. While Stu and Luke focused on the biscuits, Clara opened the fridge and took out two disks of dough — one hers, the other Luke's. The dough had chilled nicely during the time that she and Luke had been in the living room with their cocoa.

Barbara leaned over her shoulder. "Those look good."

"Thanks," Clara said.

"Are they chilled enough?"

"Yep." To Melody, she said, "Can you get the parchment paper from the top drawer there?"

Melody reached into the drawer and pulled out the parchment paper.

"Let's get the counter cleared to give you space to roll out the dough," Barbara said. Quickly, the three women moved the mixer and bowls out of the way and unrolled a generous length of parchment paper on the counter.

"Luke," Clara said, "how thick do you need your dough rolled out?"

Luke pulled his recipe card out of his back pocket to check. "About the thickness of a graham cracker."

"What about the shape?"

"Circles are best."

Clara opened an upper cabinet and pulled out a glass jar. "How about we use this?"

He eyed the jar's mouth and nodded. "Looks good."

"Okay, I'll use the same."

Barbara said to her husband, "You need help with the biscuits?"

"We're good." Stu looked at Clara, "Okay if we pop the gravy in the microwave?"

"Of course." Clara sprinkled flour over the parchment paper, unwrapped her dough disk, and started rolling. Behind her, she heard the microwave door open and shut, followed by the familiar beeps of the timer. She smiled. Plenty of men didn't know much about baking or cooking, but she'd never met a man who didn't know his way around a microwave.

The dough, nicely chilled, was holding up well under the rolling pin. Clara paused to sprinkle more flour on the roller, then got back to it. Gradually, the dough spread out over the surface of the parchment paper.

Melody picked up the jar. "Do I...?"

Clara eyed the dough, which was now just shy of a quarter inch thick. "Yep, ready. Let's make six cookies from this dough disk, then six from the other. Let me get the cookie pan."

While Melody began pressing the jar into the

dough to create six circles, Clara pulled open a lower drawer and took out a large cookie pan, which she set on the opposite counter.

Barbara slid in a piece of parchment paper. "We ready, Melody?"

Melody finished her sixth circle and stood back. "Ready." Carefully, she removed the excess dough from around the six circles. "Should we wrap up the excess dough and put it back in the fridge?"

"Yes, that'd be great," Clara said as she carefully placed the first of the six circular cookies on the cookie pan. "That way we can chill it to use later."

With cookies from the first dough disk — her disk — ready for the oven, she set to work on Luke's. Behind her, the microwave pinged and she heard one of the men open the door. Almost immediately, the wonderful aroma of hot gravy filled the kitchen.

"That smells so good," Clara said.

"Be ready in just a sec," Stu said.

Next to her, Melody noticed the cocoa still warming on the stovetop. "Clara, what is this?"

"Hot cocoa. You want some?"

"Darling, I'd love some. You sure?"

"Of course, go for it! Get yourself a mug and have at it."

Melody opened the upper cabinet and, after a moment, grabbed a mug with an important message printed it: "Never stand between a woman and her latte."

Clara grinned. "My personal motto."

Melody laughed. "Barbara, Stu, Luke, would you like some hot cocoa?"

"No thanks," Barbara said.

"Ditto," Stu said.

"Ditto," Luke added. "What about you? You want a biscuit?"

"I couldn't," Melody said. "I had two earlier this morning. If I have a third, I'll burst."

Clara finished rolling the dough and, satisfied with its thickness, used the jar to quickly make six round cookies. Without further ado, she added them to the cookie pan.

Barbara inspected the pan. "Looks like you're ready. You know which half of the pan is yours and which is Luke's?"

Clara nodded. "I do."

Barbara opened the oven door and stood aside as Clara slid the cookies in.

"How long should we set the timer for?"

Clara turned to Luke. "Luke, twelve minutes okay?"

"Yep, twelve minutes."

A thought went through Clara's head as she set the cookies in the oven and closed the oven door: She didn't really care whose cookies turned out better. Being here in this kitchen with these wonderful people was reward enough.

Nah, another voice told her. *You still wanna win.*

She grinned and turned to her guests. "Okay, folks, judging begins soon."

"Clara," Stu said, "is that table by the bay window big enough for the five of us?"

"Sure. We can pull it out a bit to give everyone enough room to slide in." Melody stepped forward and helped her pick up the table and scoot it out a bit, leaving plenty of space for folks to get to the bench in the bay window. "Let's have the judges on the bench, and Luke and I will take the two chairs so we can bring you the cookies when they're ready."

Barbara rubbed her hands together. "The only thing better than Christmas cookies — is *judging* Christmas cookies!"

Stu pointed to a chair. "Have a seat, Clara. You and Luke should rest your feet for a few minutes."

"You act like I'm an invalid," Clara protested.

"No, just a young woman who doesn't realize how hard she works."

"Listen to Stu, darling," Melody insisted. "Sit."

"Okay, fine," Clara said with a sigh as she allowed herself to be guided to a chair. As soon as she sat down, Stu slid a biscuit and steaming-hot cup of gravy in front of her.

"Dig in," he ordered.

Luke, with a plate of his own in hand, settled down next to her. "No argument from me," he said. Without hesitation, he tore off a big, flaky chunk of his biscuit and thrust it deep into the gravy cup, then shoveled the whole thing into his mouth and closed his eyes. "Mmmmm," he murmured, causing Clara to blink in pleased surprise. For just a second, she saw a glimpse of the kid he'd once been — innocently and completely enjoying the simple pleasures of great food.

Following his lead, Clara picked up her biscuit, did a deep dip into the gravy, and dug in.

Oh, my! The wonderful heat and tastes exploded in her mouth. The meaty tang of gravied ham, with just a touch of chili pepper for heat, mixed with the chewy, buttery goodness of the biscuit — so perfect.

Barbara slid into the bench seat, followed by Stu and Melody. For several long seconds, they watched Clara and Luke wolfing down the biscuits and gravy, small smiles on their faces.

"It's nice to see you two enjoying my food," Barbara said.

"Barbara, this is amazing," Luke said.

"It's so good," Clara echoed between bites.

"I agree completely," Melody said. "I have to say — I can't tell you how much I've enjoyed my time here. You've made me so welcome here."

"And we've been so happy to have you," Barbara said, reaching across her husband to take Melody's hand in hers. "Even if it is for such a short visit. I'm so sorry to hear you have to leave us first thing tomorrow morning to catch your flight to Switzerland with Derek."

A shadow passed over Melody's face, just for a second, before Melody returned the smile to her face and said brightly, "So tell us, darling. How will the cookie contest work this afternoon?"

"It's at the rec center," Barbara said, sitting back in her seat, "which is great, since the kitchen there has eight ovens and three big refrigerators and loads of prep space."

Melody's eyebrows rose. "That's a lot of ovens."

"They come in handy. The rec center is multi-purpose, with events and dinners for different organizations and events throughout the year. A couple of years ago, a bunch of us pitched in and redid the kitchen area, which was sadly outdated, and brought it into the modern era."

"Will the competitors use the kitchen to bake their cookies?"

Barbara nodded. "If they want to, yes."

Clara looked up from her plate, which now held only one delicious bite, the rest having already been inhaled. "What do you mean, if they want to?"

"Contestants have a choice: If they bake their cookies at home, they can bring the cookies with them and have an hour to do all the decorating they can. If they start the dough from scratch at the rec center, they'll have three hours."

"That makes sense," Clara said, "since some contestants need their dough to chill...."

"Like us," Luke said. The last morsels of his

biscuit and gravy were gone. He leaned back in his chair, a satisfied glow on his face.

"We'll need to think about how we want to do it."

The two planners looked at each other, each of them working through the possibilities.

"Given that we need the dough to chill," Luke said after a moment, "we could get the cookies baked beforehand, then use the hour at the rec center to get the icing made for the decorations."

"I agree," Clara said, then frowned. "The thing is, Melody has a two-o'clock chocolate-making session with Abby, and I was planning to be the camera holder...."

"I can make the dough and bake the cookies while you do that," Luke said. "Or if you want, I could be the cameraman."

Clara cocked her head. "You'd be willing to do that? Be cameraman? You sure?"

"Of course. Happy to help."

"I like that idea. I could get the cookies baked here and meet you at Abby's...."

"And then we'd head to the rec center."

Clara turned to Melody. "That okay with you?"

"Of course, darling," she murmured, then turned to Luke. "This is very kind of you."

"Really, it's no problem at all."

Barbara jumped in. "What will Abby be making?"

"Caramels, I think?" Clara said.

"Oh, wonderful. Abby is so good with those."

They dove into a discussion of Abby's chocolate shop, with Melody asking questions and Barbara answering, and were so immersed in their conversation that they didn't immediately notice the oven's buzzer.

After a few seconds, Luke blinked and sat up straighter. "Is that…?"

"Oh, gosh," Clara said.

Together, the two of them stood up, went to the oven, and peered through the glass oven door. Inside, their cookies had risen and looked perfect, with a touch of brown around the edges.

"They're ready," Clara breathed.

Luke grabbed an oven mitt, Clara opened the oven, and Luke reached in and pulled them out.

"Which half is mine?" he whispered.

"The half near your mitt," she whispered back.

Carefully, he set the pan on the counter, then leaned in for a whiff. "They smell great."

She leaned in as well, the fresh-baked aromas triggering yet more childhood memories of a younger version of herself doing the very same thing with her mom. "Wonderful," she said, then turned to their judges. "A few minutes to cool down and we'll be ready. What can we get for you? Coffee? More cocoa?"

"Could I get a glass of water?" Barbara asked. "I want your cookies to be the only taste in my mouth."

"Same for me, please," Melody said.

"Make it three," Stu added.

Luke took off the oven mitt, opened the upper cabinet, and pulled out three glasses. Once again, Clara noticed how tall and solidly built he was, and how assured and effortless his actions were. With a sharp reminder to herself to *not go there*, she turned to their judges. "Ice?"

"Tap water's just fine," Barbara said. "Don't want to freeze my taste buds." The others nodded in agreement.

Luke filled the three glasses under the tap and brought them to the judges, then returned to Clara at the counter.

"How should we do this?" he asked quietly.

"They don't know who made the cookies, so we can just bring them the pan like this and have them taste cookies from one side first and then the other."

Stu piped up. "Quit that whispering, you two. Your judges are awfully hungry!"

Clara laughed and touched the edge of the cookie pan, which was no longer hot but still warm. Just to be careful, she slipped on an oven mitt, picked up the tray, took it to the table, and set it down in front of the judges.

Five pairs of eyes stared at the twelve round sugar cookies on the pan.

"Six cookies are mine and six are Luke's," Clara said.

"But you aren't going to tell us which until after we're done judging?" Melody asked.

"Exactly,"

Clara felt it then — the tension rising in the room. All five of them understood the task and the stakes. Finally, the moment of truth.

Luke shot her a grin, a teasing hint of challenge in his tone. "Confident?"

She gave him her best steady stare, trying hard not to break into a smile. "Totally. You're going down, mister."

His grin widened. "May the best cookie win."

Clara turned to the judges. "Each of you may now take a cookie from the left half of the pan." That side was hers, the other side Luke's.

Still standing, she and Luke held their breath as the judges got their first cookie. There was a moment's pause that everyone seemed to be aware of, and then — they took their first bites.

"Mmmm," Stu said after a long moment.

"Wonderful texture and taste," Melody said.

"Deliciously buttery," Barbara said. She winked at Clara, letting her know that not only had she figured out that the first cookie was Clara's, but that she knew the secret reason for the cookie's buttery taste.

"This is a wonderful cookie," Stu said.

"Agreed," Melody said.

"Absolutely."

Stu said, in his best TV announcer voice, "But will it top its competition?"

In unison, the three judges reached for cookies — Luke's — on the other side of the pan.

Next to her, she sensed her opponent tense up as they waited for the imminent judgment.

The three judges bit in and went silent as they allowed the cookies to fill their mouths.

"Mmmm," Stu said. "These are delicious, too."

"Completely," Melody said. After a second, a puzzled look appeared on her face. "But you know…."

Barbara was frowning. "I agree with you both — delicious." She noticed the frown on Melody's face, then leaned behind Stu and beckoned for Melody to come closer. Briefly, the two women whispered in each other's ears. Barbara then whispered in her husband's ear. After a second or two, he nodded. "I agree."

Barbara turned to Luke and Clara and said, very politely, "Can the judges look at your recipes?"

Surprised, Clara could only say, "Of course." Luke reached into his back pocket and handed over his recipe card. Clara went to the recipe box on the counter and, after flipping through for a few seconds, found the recipe and brought it to Barbara.

Together, the three judges looked at the two recipes. After a few seconds, Stu snorted and Melody let out a small gasp.

With a chuckle, Barbara turned to Clara and Luke and said, in a voice hinting at merriment, "We have a winner."

Barbara paused, letting the tension build —

Until Clara couldn't stand the suspense any longer. "Who's the winner?" she blurted out.

Barbara laughed. "You both are!"

What? Clara inhaled sharply, confused.

Next to her, Luke blinked with surprise. "What do you mean?" he asked, his bewilderment echoing hers.

"The two of you," Barbara said, "have the exact same recipe!"

CHAPTER 33

What? The same recipe? Clara's eyes widened and she turned to Luke, who was gaping at her in shock.

Barbara jumped in. "And I know why."

Clara whirled toward her. "Why? How?"

"Your recipe came from your mom, right?"

"Right."

Barbara swung her gaze to Luke. "And you got your recipe from your grandmother, right?"

"That's right," Luke said.

"Well, I know where both of them got the recipe. I know this because my own sugar-cookie recipe came from the very same person."

A light bulb went off in Clara's head as childhood memories rushed in — memories of hot summer afternoons relaxing on the big wide porch at the home of a wonderful neighbor, an older woman who had been so good to her and her mom, a woman whose very name was synonymous with the town her family had founded, centuries earlier.

"Minerva Heartsprings," Clara breathed.

Luke inhaled sharply. "Auntie Minerva and my grandma were great friends."

Barbara nodded. "As Minerva was with me."

"As she was with my mom," Clara added.

Luke exhaled, then laughed. "So that's how...."

"When I couldn't tell the difference between the two cookies," Barbara said, "at first I couldn't figure it out."

"Same with me, darling," Melody said. "The cookies weren't just equally delicious — they were *identically* delicious!"

"They both tasted really good to me," Stu said with a shrug.

"I love how this turned out — mystery solved, and everyone a winner," Clara said. She pivoted to Luke. "Congratulations on your victory."

Luke grinned. "Same to you." On an impulse, he reached out and pulled her in for a congratulatory hug — a hug that she found herself returning wholeheartedly, her arms circling his neck and pulling him in tight. As her cheek pressed against his hair, she caught a hint of his shampoo and perhaps aftershave and —

Gah!

What was she doing? She stiffened in his arms. He

noticed immediately and let her go and took a step back, an embarrassed flush on his cheeks matching the flaming heat she knew she had on hers.

"Congratulations," he said softly, his eyes darting self-consciously toward the three judges.

Clara's gaze followed. Barbara, Stu, and Melody were sitting still as statues, not moving a meddling muscle, clearly afraid to say or do anything that might disrupt what was happening. For a very long second, the five of them remained in place, silent and motionless. Then Barbara broke the spell and rubbed her hands together. "Gosh, will you look at the time? Let's help you get cleaned up."

"Yes, the time," Melody said, standing up and easing out from behind the table. "Where ever did it go?"

Suddenly everyone was in motion, picking up mugs and moving en masse toward the kitchen.

"Guys, no need to clean up anything," Clara said, relieved that everyone had decided to ignore the elephant — *elephant, ha ha* — in the room. "I've still got work to do. More cookies to make."

"You sure?" Melody asked.

"Completely. Barbara, how many cookies do we need?"

"Four dozen," Barbara said.

"Then I should get busy."

"And we should get out of your hair," Stu said.

Melody turned to Luke. "You sure about being the cameraman?"

"Of course," he said. "You need a ride to Abby's?"

"That would be great. Is it okay if we swing by the Inn first?"

"Of course."

Clara took the plastic containers that had once held the biscuits and gravy and handed them back to Stu. "Don't forget these."

"Thank you, young lady."

"No, thank *you*." To everyone, she added, "Thank you all — this was really fun."

A flurry of goodbyes and coat-gathering and hugs ensued. Before Clara knew it, Stu and Melody were out the door and Barbara was turning to Luke to say, "See you at the Inn in a few." Before they could stop her, she pulled the door shut, leaving Luke and Clara alone in the entry hallway.

The sudden silence was notable. After a pause, Luke chuckled. "Wow."

Clara grinned. "Quite the whirlwind, those three."

Luke reluctantly shrugged into his winter coat, in no hurry to leave, his blue eyes steady on her. "I'm really glad we did this."

"I'm glad, too," she replied. She was standing a bit too close to him, she realized. His handsome face, those intense blue eyes holding her gaze, his strong clean-shaven jaw — way too close for comfort. A few more inches' distance would be better — infinitely better, infinitely saner. Yet she couldn't seem to get her legs to move.

"I'm glad both our families have Auntie Minerva's recipe," he said. "Makes me feel closer to this town somehow. Like we're carrying on a Heartsprings Valley tradition."

How exactly right that was. Sometimes, the little things mattered so much. The small but important details, the everyday moments that held so much meaning, if only you noticed.

If only you noticed….

The words reverberated through her. She blinked as a flash of understanding nearly blinded her. For the first time, she saw what she hadn't been seeing. What she'd been avoiding, skirting around, pushing off, holding at bay. And not just for the past two days in Heartsprings Valley — but for months.

Luke frowned — he'd picked up right away that something was up. Unlike her, he was good at noticing. "What's going through that head of yours?"

Time. She needed time to sort this all out. Not because she was panicked, not because she was flustered or off-balance or unsure. For the first time in two days, she felt the ground beneath her becoming solid again. No, she needed time to form a plan, because that was how she was wired, plain and simple. What she wanted to do was important. It was important to do it right.

"I'm fine," she said, staring up at the quizzical

expression on his face. "I just realized something, that's all."

"What's that?"

She smiled. "Can I tell you in a bit, after we win the cookie contest? Just a bit of planning I realized I need to get done."

He held her gaze for a long second, affection and patience in his eyes. "Guess I should get going."

She nodded. "Guess so."

"Gotta go film a Broadway star making chocolates," he said with a chuckle. "Two days ago, if you'd asked me what I'd be doing on Christmas Eve...."

"I know. Crazy."

He gestured toward the kitchen. "You okay with the dough and the cookies?"

"With Auntie Minerva's recipe, we can't lose."

"Good. I like the sound of that. I want us to *win* this contest."

"We will." She patted him on the shoulder. "Now scoot. I'll join you at Abby's as soon as I can."

"You got everything for the icing? The decorations?"

"Covered. I'll bring everything we need."

"Okay." He paused at the door, as if unwilling or unable to leave her.

He wants to kiss me, her rebellious heart whispered.

She didn't even try to argue with herself. "See you

in a bit," she said, doing her best to hold herself together and speak as calmly as she could.

Understanding flickered in his blue eyes. He pulled open the door. Cold winter air rushed in. "See you in a bit." Then he turned and walked to his truck.

She watched him get in and start up and pull out, waving as he drove away. Shivering, she shut the door tight and stood in the entry hall for a long moment, lost in thought.

Yes, she told herself, what she'd just realized was right. It had taken her a long time to figure it out, but now that she had, she felt it in her bones.

Which meant she had a list to work on. There was so much to do.

Starting with a very important phone call.

CHAPTER 34

*S*he dashed back into the kitchen and got started right away. It was amazing how time seemed to fly — or maybe expand? — when she had a million things to do. There was dough to make and chill and turn into cookies and bake. A kitchen to clean up. A contest to pack ingredients and utensils for. A to-do list to create. A call to make. With clear head and full heart, she launched herself at her tasks, one after another, finding her flow as she pushed forward. She'd always had a knack for organizing — and now she was showing how efficient and effective she could be.

Two hours later, the last batch of delicious sugar cookies cooling on the counter, she allowed herself to take a deep breath. She surveyed the kitchen, satisfied that she was leaving it suitably cleaned up. The icing's ingredients, double-checked to confirm she hadn't forgotten any, were carefully packed with bowls and utensils into a shopping bag that now stood on the counter, ready to bring to the car. She'd freshened up, making sure all was good in the face and hair and clothing departments, adding a touch of lip gloss to help protect against the cold. *And maybe for another reason as well,* her rebellious inner voice teased, to which her mature voice replied, *Oh, grow up already.*

Carefully, she transferred the last of the cookies to the carrying container, then sealed the container tight and placed it in a second grocery bag. She opened the dishwasher, set the cookie sheet and spatula inside, added detergent, closed the door tight, and hit the "on" button.

As the dishwater whirred to life, she stepped to the hallway, donned her hat and gloves and coat and scarf, and returned to the kitchen for her cargo. After checking her coat pockets to make sure she had the essentials — car keys and phone and, yes, lip gloss — she picked up the two grocery bags and headed toward the front door, pausing to inspect her reflection in the entry hall mirror one final time.

Yes, the young woman staring back at her was ready for this. More than ready. With a bounce in her step, she shut the door behind her, opened the garage door, set the bags in the car, hopped behind the driver's seat, and turned the car on, smiling as the radio filled the air with a holiday classic about a certain little drummer boy.

Singing along, she pulled out of the garage and headed toward Abby's shop. The afternoon sun seemed unusually bright today — or was that just her? She couldn't help but smile as she took in the holiday favorites — reindeer and snowmen and sleds and more — decorating so many of the front yards she passed. She'd always appreciated her hometown's charms, but Heartsprings Valley seemed especially beautiful that day.

The rec center was about a block off the square, an easy walk from Abby's shop. She found a spot in front of the center and parked, then made her way down the sidewalk to the square. As she pushed through the door to Abby's shop, the delightful aroma of chocolate welcomed her. Behind the counter, a teenage girl with braces and pigtails — Ava, if she remembered right — was busy helping a customer pick out treats.

The girl glanced up. "Welcome to Abby's Chocolate Heaven! Be with you in just a minute."

"I'm here for the filming," Clara said.

"Oh, you must be Clara," Ava replied with grin. "They're waiting for you in back."

"Thank you, and merry Christmas."

"Merry Christmas to you."

Clara slipped behind the counter and through the door into the small kitchen. Abby and Melody were near the sink, setting down some bowls for cleaning. Luke was a few feet away, holding Melody's phone.

Three heads swiveled toward her.

"Clara," Melody said as she turned on the faucet. "Perfect timing. We're just wrapping up."

"How'd everything go?"

"Darling, it went wonderfully. Abby is a genius with chocolates."

Abby blushed as she said, "Clara, we've had so much fun today. Thank you so much for thinking of me — it's an adventure I'll always remember."

"So glad to hear that — but really, the thanks should be from us to you."

"Absolutely," Melody piped up.

Clara glanced over at Luke. "How'd you hold up?"

He grinned. "Tough gig, holding a phone and pressing a button. Somehow I survived. A steady supply of chocolates helped."

Clara chuckled. "You ready to win a cookie contest?"

"Ready and waiting. Let's do it."

Melody turned to Abby. "You sure we can't help clean up?"

Abby shook her head. "I've got it. If I finish up in time here, I'll see you at the cookie contest. And if not there, definitely at the Christmas concert in the square."

Melody pulled Abby in for a hug. "Thank you so much, Abby."

Abby blushed again. "The pleasure is all mine. Now scoot."

A few minutes later, after stopping at the car to pick up the grocery bags full of cookies and icing ingredients and baking utensils, the trio stepped into the rec center and were immediately swept into the rush of pre-contest activities. Barbara zoomed in on Melody and pulled her away to meet the other judges. At the same time, a young woman with a clipboard approached Luke and Clara.

"Luke," the woman said, reaching up to give him a quick peck on the cheek, "good to see you. I didn't know you were doing this." In her early thirties with shoulder-length brown hair and a warm, attractive face, the woman wore a festive red-and-white sweater and dark slacks.

"Me neither," he replied. "Not until last night." He glanced at Clara. "Do you two know each other?"

With a friendly smile, the woman extended her hand. "I'm Becca Shepherd, the new librarian."

"Clara Cane," Clara said, considering the woman before her. Her name rang a bell — but why? Her dad had mentioned that Hettie Mae, the town's long-time librarian, had retired. Had he also mentioned the name of Hettie Mae's successor?

Then it came. With a small gasp, Clara exclaimed, "You made the gingerbread house in Abby's store window — that adorable gingerbread log cabin with the couple and the cat and the dog."

Becca laughed, pleased. "Just a little hobby of mine. Abby is kind enough to feature my gingerbread houses in her window display from time to time."

"You do beautiful work."

"Thank you. And you said ... Clara Cane? Any relation to Ted Cane at the hardware store?"

"My dad."

"So you're his daughter, who lives in New York? Welcome home."

"Thank you."

"I'm new here — barely a year — so I'm still getting to know everyone."

Luke jumped in. "Becca just got married to my buddy Nick."

"Congratulations," Clara said.

"Thank you," Becca said, glowing like the newlywed she was.

"Speaking of Nick, where is he?" Luke asked.

"At the clinic. A neighbor brought in a cat who's not feeling well. He'll get here when he can." To Clara, she added, "Nick's a veterinarian."

Clara had already figured as much. "Does he run his practice out of the old Heartsprings mansion?"

"That's right," Becca said.

My, my — how tightly woven was the fabric of life in Heartsprings Valley. Once again, Clara felt its tug.

Becca glanced at her watch. "Gosh, look at the time. Let's get you to your work space." She led them across the main room, where folks were setting up rows of folding chairs to face the stage, then through swinging double doors into the kitchen prep area in the back.

As they stepped in, Clara's eyes widened. The space was bigger than she'd remembered, with ovens, sinks, and granite counters lining the walls and huge islands near each corner of the room.

"Wow," Clara said. "Barbara mentioned that the space has been updated, but this is amazing."

Becca nodded. "It's a perfect prep area for events like this." She guided them to a countertop on the far wall. "Here's your space."

"Looks great," Luke said.

"You got what you need?" Becca said.

Luke gestured to the two grocery bags he was carrying. "All set."

"Good." Becca glanced at her watch again. "You have until five-thirty to finish your decorating."

"What happens then?" Clara asked.

"The judges will be up on stage. A pair at a time, the contestants will join them onstage, introduce their cookies to the audience, and share their cookies with the judges. After evaluating the entries for taste and presentation, the judges will announce the winners.

All the contestants will then share their remaining cookies — we've asked for four dozen cookies from each pair of contestants — with the crowd."

"Quite a show," Luke said.

Becca gazed at the two of them, a big grin on her face. "Events like this make me so glad I moved to Heartsprings Valley." She glanced again at her watch. "Oh, gosh — I've got a billion things to do. Any questions, just ask. Good luck with your cookies!"

"Thanks!" Clara said, watching Becca bustle off.

Luke turned to the grocery bags. "We have enough time?"

"Not as much as we'd like," Clara said, "so we'll just have to make do." Reaching into a bag, she pulled out a sheet of paper and a pencil. "Given the time factor, we're best off painting icing directly onto the cookies. We can draw ideas first to figure out what we want."

Luke started unpacking the bags. "I was thinking…. It would be great if Auntie Minerva could somehow be our guide."

"Oh, I like that. We can decorate the cookies in ways reflecting our memories of her. And we can call our cookies 'Minervas.'"

Luke grinned. "Love it." With the ingredients lined up on the counter, he pulled a big mixing bowl from the bottom of the bag. "You want me to start the icing?"

"Sure. You know how to do it?"

"I think so," he said, pulling his recipe card out of his back pocket. "Do these instructions look good?"

She quickly perused the card. "Yes, perfect."

"Okay. I'll ask if I have questions."

She watched him measure out the confectioners' sugar, then turned her attention to the sheet of paper. After drawing a circle the size of a cookie, she started experimenting with shapes and lines, allowing herself to be inspired by the joy of Christmas and her memories of Auntie Minerva. After a few false starts, the ideas started flowing. The pencil and paper yielded drawings of holiday ornaments, Christmas trees, beautifully wrapped gifts, and a few happy snowmen for good measure. Auntie Minerva had loved animals, so Clara found herself drawing a picture of a cute dog wearing a Santa cap and a cat curled up near a roaring fire. Finally, she drew a side profile of Minerva herself, her bearing erect, her chin firm, a holiday brooch on her dress. Along the bottom of the circle, she added the words, "Merry Christmas! Love, Minerva."

Luke peered over her shoulder. "These look great."

She glanced up. "How's the icing coming?"

"Added in the egg whites, cream of tartar, and kosher salt." He pointed to a mixer on the counter, which even now was whirring away. "Mixing it now."

"Perfect. You know what we're going to need…."

"More icing?"

She nodded.

"I'll get that started."

CHAPTER 35

*T*hey were a good team, the two of them. Instinctively, without needing to consult one another, they seemed to know how to divvy up the work. As he had that morning, Luke applied care and precision to his tasks, measuring out the ingredients carefully before adding them to the mixing bowl.

He pointed to the container full of food coloring she'd brought with her. "How many colors will we be using?"

She looked at the designs she'd penciled out and started counting. Red and green and white were givens, of course. Touches of yellow and black would be needed as well, along with blue. "We'll start with white and five colors and go from there."

She'd brought more than enough food coloring and more than enough plastic bags, so she wasn't concerned about a lack of color. But a lack of time —

that was a different story. If they were going to win this thing, they'd have to become decorating monsters.

All around them, the other contestants were busy as well. Most had brought their baked cookies with them and were busy decorating, but several teams were pulling freshly baked cookies out of ovens, the wonderful aromas wafting in the air.

Clara opened her cookie container, breathing in the fresh-baked scent. Choosing to make round cookies had been a good move — the circle shape ensured the cookies had baked evenly, and also provided a big canvas for the icing they'd soon be painting on them.

She took a cookie from the container and set it on a plate, then consulted her drawings. She hadn't done this in a while — years, in fact — so she started with the easiest design to make sure she still had the hang of it. Which meant the first cookie would be … a snowman. The base color would be white, his eyes and button nose would be black, his mouth red, and his corncob pipe yellow. His top hat would be black, with a ribbon of green.

She sighed, realizing where she was going with this. Five colors, for one cookie? And this was the simple design?

"What's the matter?" Luke asked.

"I'm insane," she sighed. "This is way too ambitious. We'll never get this done."

He frowned and looked at the snowman design. "Nah, we'll be fine. You focus on finishing one cookie of each design. Once I know what to do, I can bang these out and so can you."

She was glad she was doing this with him. "I like your optimism."

He shrugged. "We'll adjust as needed as the clock ticks down."

Confidence restored, she grabbed the bowl of icing that Luke had already finished and scooped a third of it into a second bowl. She selected the black food coloring and added in a generous amount, then grabbed a whisk and mixed it in. Very quickly, the white icing turned gray. She added more food coloring and mixed it more, and then threw in a third splash for good measure.

The icing was dark now — not pitch black, but definitely a coal gray. She scooped several healthy spoonfuls into a plastic bag, pressing the icing through the bag so that it gathered in one corner. Using a knife, she snipped off the tip of the corner, then held the piping bag over the cookie and started painting on the snowman's eyes and nose and coat buttons and top hat.

Yes, she thought, surveying her first cookie, this could work. She scooped more white icing into a third bowl, mixed in yellow food coloring, trans-ferred the golden icing to a third bag, then carefully added the snowman's corncob pipe.

"Keep the icing coming," she said to Luke. "We're gonna need a lot of it."

"More on the way."

"How much time do we have left?"

"Forty-four minutes."

The first cookie — her test-case snowman — ended up taking the longest, in large part because Clara was mixing the initial batches of color. Once the bowls and plastic bags were set up for each color, her pace picked up.

Quicker than she would have thought possible, she finished the first cookie for each of the eight designs she'd painted onto cookies: two ornaments, a Christmas tree, a stack of gifts, a dog, a cat, a snowman, and the side profile of Auntie Minerva. The colors were bold, the lines simple, and the subjects heartwarmingly traditional.

"These look great," Luke said, watching her finish writing "Minerva" on the first Auntie Minerva cookie. "They tell a story."

She nodded, pleased. "They do, don't they?"

Becca bustled up to them. "My, those are pretty!" she said, then tapped her watch. "Twenty-eight minutes."

"Yikes!" Clara said.

"We got this," Luke said as he picked up a cookie and a plastic bag. "We have all the time in the world."

There was no time to disagree, so Clara got to work beside him, their paces gradually picking up.

Together, as the clock wound down, they finished a dozen more cookies, and then another dozen.

Clara glanced at the wall clock. Three minutes. She turned to Luke. "I'm going to plate the best dozen for the judges."

"Go for it." He was moving fast now, in a rhythm of purpose, his precision and focus enabling him to whip out new cookies astonishingly quickly.

From a grocery bag, she pulled out her favorite serving plate. It was oval in shape, a crisp white porcelain, an heirloom inherited from her mom. Quickly, without allowing herself to overthink, she zeroed in on the best dozen cookies and added them to the serving tray. The cookies looked so colorful together, the designs playing off each other wonderfully.

"Two minutes," she heard Becca yell out.

Luke was closing in on the final unfinished cookies, his hands racing from bag to cookie to bag.

Gosh, it was going to be close. Glancing at the serving plate, she realized that something was missing. But what? She frowned, pondering, then — yes! She picked up the red icing and wrote, along the bottom edge of the plate, "Merry Christmas! Love, Auntie Minerva."

"Thirty seconds," Becca yelled.

"Yikes!" Clara exclaimed again.

Luke sped up even more, turning into a crazy cookie-decorating speed demon. He looked like he'd been doing this for years, his competitive spirit pushing him — and her — to new heights.

"Ten seconds," Becca said, then counted down as Luke zeroed in on the final cookie, adding first one color and then another and —

"Time!" Becca yelled out. "Contestants, step away from your cookies."

CHAPTER 36

*L*uke raised his hands and stepped back and blinked as if dazed and coming out of a trance.

Clara looked at the cookies laid out before her. Every single one was decorated!

"Luke, you did it," she exclaimed.

He took a deep breath and then another, his eyes taking in the completed cookies like he didn't believe it either. "We made it?"

"The cookies look terrific."

She reached out and pulled him in for a hug — which he immediately returned.

"I can't believe we pulled this off," he said.

His strong arms felt wonderful around her. But gradually she became aware of her surroundings and pulled back.

Sensing that, he disengaged, but his gaze

remained fixed on her.

In the center of the room, Becca said, "Contestants, let's gather together for a sec." Clara and Luke stepped away from their cookies and joined the other contestants.

"First of all, congratulations to all of you for taking part in today's contest. Give yourselves a big round of applause." The contestants clapped appreciatively, and Becca continued. "The contest starts in just a minute. Our head judge, Barbara, will introduce the judges and then invite each team onto the stage. When it's your turn, please briefly introduce yourselves and your cookies. No long speeches, okay? This audience is hungry! After the judges announce the winner, everyone should feel free to share their cookies with the audience."

Becca reached into a bag at her feet and pulled out a small plastic trophy showing two gold figures in baker's aprons standing proudly together, arms crossed. "This, of course, is what you're competing for: the winners' trophy for the Heartsprings Valley Christmas Cookie Contest."

Luke leaned down and whispered in Clara's ear, "I want that trophy soooo bad."

"Shush," she whispered back, stifling a giggle. Though if she was being honest, she wanted that trophy, too!

"So that's the plan, folks," Becca said. "Good luck."

Four pairs preceded Clara and Luke. As they

awaited their turn, Clara stood nervously at the door, her stomach clenched in knots.

Luke, as observant as ever, said, "Hey, no need to worry. We got this covered."

"How about you introduce us, and I'll bring the cookies to the judges' table?"

"You sure? I'm good either way."

"Yes, I'm sure."

Becca's voice, now piping up over the loud-speaker, came through loud and clear. "Please welcome our next pair — Clara Cane and Luke Matthews."

Plate in hand, Clara stepped into the main room and onto the small stage, Luke a step behind her. The judges were lined up behind a table on the far end of the stage. There were five of them — a man and two women she didn't know, along with Barbara and Melody, both grinning at her.

Clara swung the cookie plate toward the audience to let them see it, then brought the plate to the judges.

Luke stepped to the microphone and said, "Hi, everyone. When Clara and I got maneuvered into doing this contest together" — his choice of words inspiring chuckles from the audience, most of whom understood perfectly well what Heartsprings Valley was capable of — "we didn't agree about which recipe to use. I wanted to go with my grandma's recipe, and Clara wanted to go with her mom's. So we agreed on a bake-off this morning to decide the winner."

He paused, knowing he had the crowd with him. "We ended up both baking really delicious sugar cookies. And the winner ended up being — both of us!"

The audience exchanged puzzled looks: How could both of them be the winner?

With a grin, Luke continued. "The recipes, it turns out, were exactly the same. And the reason for that? My grandma and Clara's mom both inherited their amazing sugar-cookie recipe from the same wonderful friend: Minerva Heartsprings."

At that, the crowd murmured appreciatively. "So in recognition of Auntie Minerva's enduring legacy here in Heartsprings Valley, we're calling our cookies 'Minervas.' We hope you enjoy them."

The crowd clapped warmly, their affection for their departed neighbor easy to see in their faces.

As Clara set the plate on the judges' table, Barbara gave her a wink. "Good job, Clara. You've chosen well."

"Thank you," Clara replied, aware that Barbara was referring to more than just the cookies.

Clara followed Luke off the stage as Becca announced the next pair of contestants. She watched the judges taking bites, jotting down notes, and discussing the entries quietly among themselves. There hadn't been a lot of time to check out the competition — okay, there hadn't been any time at all — but she saw now that they were up against some really terrific-looking cookies.

As the final pair of contestants exited the stage, Becca took the microphone. "Everyone, a round of applause for our wonderful contestants." She turned to the judges. "Judges, you've seen and tasted some terrific cookies today. Do you have the winner?"

At the judges table, Barbara looked at each judge in turn, pointed at a notecard in her hand, and waited for each of them to nod in confirmation. Then she stood up and joined Becca at stage center. She took the microphone and said, "First of all, the five of us have so enjoyed being your judges today. Everyone did such a wonderful job with their cookies — you've made our decision very difficult."

She paused to clear her throat. "Before I announce the winner, I'd like to thank our guest judge, who came all the way from New York City to be part of today's contest. Everyone, please give a big Heartsprings Valley welcome to the lovely and talented star of stage and screen, Melody Connelly!"

The crowd rose to their feet, clapping heartily, causing Melody to blush and blink rapidly, as if batting away tears. She stood and bowed and waved, clearly touched by the warmth of the crowd's welcome.

"And now," Barbara said, "the moment of truth."

The audience went quiet, awaiting the results with bated breath.

"This was a difficult decision, but it was unanimous. The winner of this year's Heartsprings Valley Christmas Cookie Contest is —"

She paused dramatically — Melody had been right about Barbara having natural stage presence — before saying:

"Clara Cane and Luke Matthews!"

CHAPTER 37

*C*lara gasped. Next to her, Luke whooped with delight, just like he'd done back in high school when his football team won a big game.

All around them, the crowd was on their feet, applauding enthusiastically.

Through a haze of shock and disbelief, she saw that Becca and Barbara were gesturing for her to join them onstage. But her legs weren't cooperating. Suddenly it was hard to breathe. She blinked, her brain trying to make sense of what had just happened.

Then, like she had been waiting for it all along, she felt Luke's hand on the small of her back, gently guiding her to the stage.

Time seemed to speed up. Before she knew it, Becca placed the trophy in her hands and Barbara said, "Congratulations to our winners!" At the judges' table, Melody gave her a grin and a thumb's up.

Luke turned her to face him, a huge grin on his face, clearly as amazed as she was.

"We did it," he said.

"I can't believe this is happening," she managed to get out.

He pulled her in for a hug. "Me neither." Then he laughed and held her tighter as the crowd applauded even more loudly.

She didn't want the moment to end — why was everything moving so fast? — but the hug ended before she knew it as she and Luke were surrounded by folks rushing up to offer their congratulations. She found herself saying "Thank you" and "Of course, happy to share Auntie Minerva's recipe" over and over again to well-wishers.

She heard Luke's voice in her ear and turned to find him standing in front of her with two plates of cookies — *their* cookies. "Time to share," he said, handing her a plate. Gently, he aimed her right into the center of the crowd, where an eager army waited to taste this year's winner.

As hands reached in and cookies vanished, she heard Barbara calling her name and turned to see her bustling toward her.

With a worried expression on her face, Barbara leaned in and whispered in Clara's ear, "Something's up with Melody."

Startled, Clara felt the shock of winning vanish. "What do you mean?"

"She just told me she has to leave town right away."

Clara frowned. "I thought she was leaving tomorrow morning to get back to New York in time for her flight to Switzerland."

"Not now." Barbara nodded over Clara's shoulder, and Clara turned to see Melody slipping out the door.

"What about the Christmas concert? She seemed so excited to be part of that."

"I don't know, dear."

Instantly, Clara knew what she had to do. She held out the plate of cookies. "Can you take this? Tell Luke I'll be back in a bit. I need to find out what's up."

"Of course," Barbara said.

Without wasting another second and not even bothering to find her winter coat, Clara dashed outside. Where had Melody gone? Why had she left so suddenly? Darkness had fallen while they'd been busy inside. Clouds blanketed the sky overhead, obscuring the moon and stars. Cold, sharp air filled her lungs and penetrated her shirt. On the sidewalk ahead of her, fading into the gloom, she caught sight of her client's tall, slim figure hurrying away.

"Melody!" she called out. "Wait a sec!"

Her client kept moving away at a rapid pace, forcing Clara to break into a trot to chase after her.

"Melody," she said when she finally caught up. "Stop walking so fast! I want to talk."

Melody's jaw clenched, as if she were struggling with a decision. She glanced briefly at Clara, took a deep breath, and stopped dead in her tracks, her body rigid, keeping her eyes fixed on a distant point.

"Melody," Clara said, pausing for breath, trying to read the tense expression on Melody's face. "What's this about you needing to leave before the concert?"

"I have to, darling." Her client tried to deliver the line with her usual energy and charm, but the words sounded hollow and brittle. "And what are you doing outside without your coat? You should get back inside."

"I thought you didn't have to head back until tomorrow morning to catch your flight to Switzerland."

Her client didn't answer, but Clara noticed her lip trembling with suppressed emotion.

Clara moved in front of Melody and looked straight up at her beautiful, talented client. "I'm worried about you."

"No need to worry, darling. I'm fine."

Clara took Melody's hands in hers, doing her best to coax those famous green eyes to look back at her. "Melody, I want to know what's going on." When

Melody didn't respond, she asked what she really wanted to know:

"Why did you come to Heartsprings Valley?"

For several long seconds, Melody remained silent. Then, finally, as if surrendering to reality, she returned Clara's gaze and exhaled. "Because it was Christmas and I had nowhere else to be."

Clara frowned. "Nowhere else? What about Derek? What about your family?"

"My family," Melody said, swallowing hard, "is just me and my mom. We love each other but we aren't close, for too many reasons to go into now. Maybe someday, over a bottomless bottle of wine, I'll share the whole messy story."

"Where is your mom right now?"

"On a cruise," Melody said tightly. "With husband number four."

"Oh," Clara said.

"Like I said. Messy."

"I'm sorry."

A tear rolled down Melody's cheek. Breaking loose of Clara's hands, she angrily brushed the tear away. "The cruise is my fault. I paid for her to go — my Christmas gift to her. She wanted to come to New York to spend Christmas with me. But I told her no, because I was going to Switzerland with Derek." She let out a short, pained laugh. "Derek."

"What about Derek?" Clara asked.

A long sigh escaped Melody's lips. Tears rolled

down her cheeks as the truth finally came out. "He dumped me. Four days ago. Told me he met someone else."

"Oh, Melody, I'm so sorry," Clara said, pulling her in for a hug.

"I'm sorry, too," Melody replied, her voice ragged in Clara's ear. "I'm sorry I didn't see it coming. I should have, but I didn't. I was so caught up in the idea of us that I missed the reality of us. And the reality was that he's not right for me and I'm not right for him."

"I'm so sorry." For four long days, this poor woman had maintained a nearly perfect facade. How difficult it must have been to keep all that disappointment and sadness bottled up inside.

Melody pulled back from the hug and wiped her cheeks again. "I should be used to this by now. After all —" another angry laugh — "it's what I wanted, right?"

"What do you mean?"

"I left everything and everyone behind— willingly — when I moved to New York. I worked so hard for so many years and didn't look back, not even for a second." She exhaled, her voice full of regret. "It's only after achieving everything I've spent my entire life chasing that I'm beginning to understand what I gave up."

"And by 'what,' am I sensing you also mean 'who'?"

Melody nodded. "A terrific guy. I thought he was the one. But I broke it off. Karma, right?"

The poor thing.... "If you aren't flying off to Switzerland tomorrow, what are you going to do?"

Melody shook her head. "Hide in my apartment under a blanket, order takeout, watch old movies with a big bottle of wine, and not answer the phone."

Clara's entire body tensed. *That* was Melody's plan? Really?

"No," Clara said.

"No?"

"No no no. You're doing nothing of the sort."

"What do you mean?"

She reached out and again took Melody's hands in hers. "You're going to stay here and spend Christmas with me and my dad. And not as my client."

Surprise flashed in Melody's eyes. "What do you mean, not as your client?"

"You'll be spending Christmas with us as my *friend*."

Melody's eyes teared up again. "Thank you, Clara." She pulled Clara in for another hug. "*Friend*. I love the sound of that. It means so much to hear you say that."

After a deep breath to steady herself, Melody pulled back and held Clara's shoulders at arm's length so she could look her new friend square in the face. "We need to get you back inside. You're shivering, poor thing. But you need to hear this first."

Clara realized she was shivering. "I need to hear what?"

"You know how amazing you are, don't you?"

Even as the cold threatened to penetrate her bones, Clara felt her face flame pink. "Melody, I —"

"No, let me finish. In the months I've known you, you've shown me nothing but kindness and patience, even when I haven't deserved much of either." Again Clara tried to protest, but Melody shushed her and continued. "You and your dad and your wonderful friends have welcomed me with open arms — I will always be so grateful for that. I hope you know how blessed you are to have them in your life."

"I do," Clara said, tears now threatening her as well. "I know that."

"They certainly know how lucky they are to have you in theirs."

"And you say that because?"

Melody chuckled. "Because I've heard how they talk about you. Especially a certain someone."

A flare of hope — insistent and apparently untamable — surged inside Clara. As carefully as she could manage, she said, "What do you mean, a certain someone?"

Melody raised a skeptical eyebrow. "Don't even try that. You know exactly who."

When Melody didn't say more, Clara was unable to stop herself from asking, "Well, what did he say?"

A small smile flashed on her client's — no, her *friend's* — beautiful face. "Let's go to the tape, shall we?" She moved to Clara's side, pulled out her phone, tapped a few buttons, and positioned the screen so that both of them could see it.

The phone showed video footage from that afternoon's chocolate-making session in Abby's shop. Luke was the cameraman, aiming the camera at Melody and Abby, who were busy finishing their truffles.

Melody, deep in meddling mode, looked mischievously at the camera and said, "Luke, that Clara sure is something special, isn't she?"

Luke cleared his throat, probably deciding how annoyed he should be at her question. "She sure is."

"You like her, don't you?"

There was a tiny pause — possibly because he was surprised at Melody's boldness, possibly because he was debating whether to call her out for her meddling — before he said, very simply, "Yeah, I do."

"A lot, right?"

Another tiny pause, and then: "That's right. A lot."

"Enough to chase after her?"

"What do you mean?"

"What if she isn't ready to leave New York?"

"Easy," he said without hesitation. "If she wants

to stay in the Big Apple, then I guess I'll be getting to know the Big Apple."

Clara inhaled with surprise. "I can't believe he said that."

Melody grinned. "Aren't you happy I asked him?"

"No!" Clara said. "Okay, yes. I mean, no. But yes."

Melody laughed. "So tell me. How does my *friend* Clara Cane feel about what she just heard?"

Despite the cold night air, Clara felt her cheeks flame red. "I think you know."

Melody gave her a tender look. "Yes, I think I do."

"I'm really glad you came up here for Christmas, Melody. I'm even more glad you're staying."

"I am, too." Suddenly, Melody went rigid and gasped. "The Christmas concert in the square! When is it?"

"Right about now. We've got time to get there — just — if we hustle."

"Then lead the way, Clara Cane — lead the way!"

CHAPTER 38

*A*s a holiday tradition, the annual Christmas concert in the town square was a must-see, must-do, must-listen, better-not-miss-it event. There was something so special and magical about the way a group of ordinary townspeople came together every year and became a singing troupe whose faithful renditions of holiday classics brought joy to all who listened.

From her vantage point in the crowd, it looked to Clara like concert attendance was higher than ever this year due to the presence of a certain Broadway star who now stood on the small stage with Bert Winters and the town choir, holding the audience spellbound with her powerful *a cappella* rendition of "Silent Night." Effortlessly, Melody's beautiful voice soared into the crisp night sky, the emotion of the song sending shivers down Clara's spine.

As the final note reverberated, not a person stirred, as if the crowd was conspiring to extend the moment. Then, with a collective explosion, the audience erupted into heartfelt applause. Melody grinned and bowed and handed the microphone to Bert, who looked at the crowd and said, "Now, how about something up-tempo?"

As Melody and the choir began showing the crowd how much they loved Rudolph the red-nosed reindeer, Clara glanced at her dad, who was standing next to her with Peggy. The two of them had their arms around each other, leaning together for warmth. They looked good together — like they'd found the right person to share the next chapter of their lives with. Next to them was Abby, and next to her were Barbara and Stu, all of them singing along joyfully with the crowd.

She felt Luke return to her side before she saw him. On some level, she realized she'd always been attuned to his presence. He'd gone to find his mom and dad, and now he was back.

"Hey," he said softly in her ear.

She looked up at his handsome face, at the blue eyes now gazing at her with fondness and so much more, and knew it was time for her to do what it was time for her to do. With a flutter in her heart, she reached out and took his gloved hand in hers. "I have something to tell you," she said. Soundlessly, she led him through the crowd and away from the concert, down the path that led to the other side of the town square, the energetic voices of the Christmas choir mixing with the crunch of their boots on fresh-fallen snow. As she came to a stop next to a gaggle of happy snowpeople, she realized, with a glance overhead, that the clouds had vanished, clearing the way for the stars twinkling in the night sky.

She turned to face her cookie-contest partner, her hand still in his. "I want you to be the first to know."

He nodded, waiting for her to speak, his eyes not once leaving hers.

"I'm taking a new job."

His eyebrows rose. "A new job?"

"Town manager."

"Town manager?"

"For the town of Heartsprings Valley."

She saw surprise flash in his eyes, followed by a huge grin that transformed his face. "For real? Tell me this is for real."

"For real."

With a loud, happy whoop, he pulled her in for a huge hug, picking her up and twirling her around effortlessly. "Best news ever!"

She laughed and said in mock protest, "Put me down, you big goof!"

He set her down, but his arms stayed around her waist. Eyes locked on her, he clearly had no intention of letting her go. She reached up and wrapped her arms behind his neck, his strength filling her with both excitement and reassurance.

"Is this what you were up to this afternoon?" he said, gazing at her with wonder. "Planning this big change?"

She nodded. "I called Mayor Winters. He's creating a new town manager position, and I knew he wanted me to apply."

"Mayor Winters just became my favorite politician ever." He leaned closer, his eyes filled with happiness. "Now — tell me why." He paused. "Are you moving because of — me?"

"Yes," she said simply, holding his gaze. "And also because of *me*."

"Meaning…?"

She pulled him closer, her cheek brushing his. "I realized something today. Something important. I wasn't giving New York my all. On some level I knew that already. But until today, I didn't understand why."

"Tell me why," he said softly in her ear.

"Because I'm ready to come home." She took a deep breath and continued. "Because I now understand, more than ever, how lucky I was to have the childhood I had, to have the dad I have, to have had the mom I had. The memories that used to bring me so much pain are now something more — a source of comfort as well. What I realized today is that I'm ready to embrace the past and return to where I belong — Heartsprings Valley."

He growled softly. "Right away, I hope."

She laughed, loving how his arms felt around her. "Soon enough. Sometime this spring. I can't leave Nigel in the lurch, or our clients. I'll stay in New York long enough to hire and train my replacement, and then…."

"You'll move home to Heartsprings Valley."

He pulled back just far enough to allow him to gaze upon her once again. From the adoring, tender look in his eyes, she knew that, from this point on, her plans would be *their* plans.

"Merry Christmas, Clara," he whispered, his voice husky with emotion.

"Merry Christmas, Luke."

Then they kissed, neither of them able to hold back even a second longer, their hearts racing and spirits soaring as they realized they had found their way home.

THE END

SWEET APPLE CHRISTMAS

A HEARTSPRINGS VALLEY SWEET ROMANCE (BOOK 3)

A perfect recipe for Christmas romance!

Cafe owner Holly Snow makes the best scones in town and accepts her single status — until a handsome orchard owner walks in and sparks begin to fly….

GET A FREE STORY!

Nick and the
Snowplow

A heartwarming holiday story about a handsome veterinarian and the shy, beautiful librarian he meets on Christmas Eve....

Nick and the Snowplow is a companion to *Christmas to the Rescue!*, the first novel in the Heartsprings Valley Winter Tale series. In *Christmas to the Rescue!*, a young librarian named Becca gets caught in a blizzard on Christmas Eve, finds shelter with a handsome veterinarian named Nick, and ends up experiencing the most surprising, adventure-filled night of her life.

Nick and the Snowplow, told from Nick's point of view, shows what happens after Nick brings Becca home at the end of their whirlwind evening.

This story is available FOR FREE when you sign up for Anne Chase's email newsletter.

Go to AnneChase.com to sign up and get your free story.

ABOUT THE AUTHOR

Greetings! I grew up in a small town (pop: 2,000) and now live in the bustling Bay Area. I write romances and mysteries, including:

The *Heartsprings Valley* romances: Celebrating love at Christmas in a small New England town.

The *Eagle Cove Mysteries:* An inquisitive cafe owner gets dragged into in murder and mayhem.

The *Emily Livingston Mysteries:* Intrigue and danger amidst the glamour and beauty of Europe.

My email newsletter is a great way to find out about upcoming books. Go to **AnneChase.com** to sign up.

Thank you for being a reader!

Printed in Great Britain
by Amazon

18810190R00174